IF I HAD YOU

VIOLET HAZE

Stoked Publishing House

Front Cover Design by Natasha Snow
ISBN-13: 978-0-9992261-1-7
Stoked Publishing House
First Edition: May 2020

A Note from Violet

This second chance romance involves a heroine who had an abortion at sixteen and the boy (now a man) who loved her but didn't understand why she would make such a decision because he wanted to take care of her. We all live, grow, and change, and I hope you enjoy the story even if it does seem like Zach is an asshole at first because above all, he loves Darcy and wants the best for her.

This story plays with the *what if she made a different decision* but I hope you'll agree by the end that she made the right choice for herself, just as every other woman who makes this decision does. Thanks for reading & enjoy!

PART I
WHAT IS

DARCY

When I first spot him in the bookstore, I'm not sure it's him.

I know that even if the guy I see is him, I shouldn't bother to make sure, and I definitely shouldn't approach him. Turning around and walking away, perhaps even leaving the store, is better than him seeing me.

Ten years since we've laid eyes on one another.

Since what might've been never came to be.

Since he told me how much his seventeen-year-old self hated me and the decision I made.

Little did he know I hated myself and the pain I caused him.

I never wanted to make him hurt, or make the decisions I did but hadn't felt as if I'd had a real choice.

But he hadn't cared, and he disappeared.

Ten years, though.

What are the chances he'd live in the same city I do now, thousands of miles from where we last were in the same place?

I have to look.

My feet start moving at the thought.

The man stands in one of the aisles, his stare intense where it's focused on the back of the book in his hand, and I'm suddenly short of breath as I take in his profile.

His dirty blond hair, which used to be to his chin and irritated the shit out of his father, is now cropped short and spiky. He might be another inch or two taller than what he was at seventeen, but he's definitely more broad-shouldered and built. It's been so long I can't be sure if it's really him, not without staring him straight in the face, but when he starts to turn toward me, I dart into the next aisle.

After a few moments he strides past, and I follow him as quietly as I can.

From behind him at a safe distance, I wonder how I'll be able to tell if it's him or not. Maybe he'll stop and talk to someone, and I can see from another side or something.

I just want to know and then I'll walk away. Well, that's what I tell myself at least.

Because it means he's alive and well, I have

wondered about him through the years. More in the years following his departure, but less as the years have passed. You know, since at some point, you have to let go.

Or so my therapist has told me repeatedly.

Lost in my thoughts, I don't realize I've lost him until I turn a corner, and he's not there.

"Shit."

Looking around, perhaps more frantically than is appropriate, I'm ready to give up until I see the restrooms straight ahead. Figuring that's where he went, I head toward them, and right as I'm about to open the women's door, a hand covers my mouth from behind.

I'm propelled forward through the door, and released once inside as the door shuts and locks, an all too familiar voice barking, "Why the fuck are you following me?"

Frozen in shock as memories and recognition flow through me, I'm not able to turn around, and I quickly realize he doesn't know who I am.

"Is Erica having you follow me to get dirt?" After I don't answer, all while wondering who the hell Erica is, he growls, "Turn around and fucking look at me. Or do you only engage in shady shit?"

Now that I know it's him, I don't want him to see who I am. Refusing to turn around, I stare at the ugly yellow tiled wall as I say, "I—I don't know anyone named Erica."

"No? Why the hell are you following me then?"

I blatantly lie in hopes the fact he doesn't seem to recognize my voice will work to my advantage. "I wasn't."

"I hate people who lie to me. I know you were following me, so out with it, before I have the store call security."

Taking a deep breath, my eyes slam shut as I say, "I thought you were somebody I knew. You're not. I'm sorry. Please just go."

"I will when you turn around." After a moment, I shiver as he steps closer to me, his warmth heating my back. "Right now."

Compressing my lips to quell the sob wanting to burst forth, I give him what he wants because he won't go away until I do, slowly turning around and lifting my teary gaze until it meets his annoyed one.

I know I look different from how I did at sixteen — my dark red hair is now shoulder-length, my glasses have been replaced with contacts, and my freckles are lighter — but it doesn't take long for his beautiful blue gaze to turn irate.

"Darcy fucking Bechel," he snarls, taking a quick step back as his gaze swipes me from head to toe. "Of all the people in the world, fucking really?"

"Hello Zachary," I whisper, my green eyes dropping away from his to stare at the floor, and my hands clasping in front of me. "I...I..."

"Don't speak." His command is harsh, his words harsh as his right hand touches my chin and he forces me to look at him. "Nothing except lies came out of your mouth then, and it doesn't appear as if that's changed any."

I grit my teeth at that, and flat out ignore him, frowning as I ask, "Who is Erica and why would someone follow you?"

"Not that it's any of your business," he replies as he steps closer until I'm backed against a wall. "But Erica is my wife, and she always thinks I'm cheating on her."

At the mention of him being married, I stiffen and move to flatten my palms on the wall to steady myself as I ask the obvious while his eyes sear into mine. "Are you?"

"Not yet."

Something in his answer causes my heart to race, and I slam my eyes shut. "You should let me go."

"Yeah?" When I manage to nod, he chuckles, its wicked intensity matching the heat of his form as he traps me completely and brings his mouth close to mine. "You'd like that, wouldn't you, if I just let you go. But I'm not going to."

One of his hands cups my cheek, the other sliding to grope my ass as he grinds his lower body into me, and a whimper slips through my barely parted lips at his touch.

"What we're going to do," he murmurs after pressing a soft kiss on my mouth, "is leave this room, quietly exit the store, and get into my car. Then, you're going to give me directions to your place, and once there, we're going to have an overdue chat. Got it?"

Anxious words fall from my tingling lips even as I keep my eyes closed. "I'm sorry I followed you. Walk away, pretend you never saw me and I'll pretend I never saw you. Please."

"I can't." He sounds tortured, his words hoarse as the hand on my ass falls to my side, and he grips my hand in his. "Let's go."

It's wrong, even as he steps away, unlocking the door and opening it, tugging me along behind him as we leave the bathroom, and through the store.

I know I should run as his clasp on my hand tightens while we head across the parking lot, and as we reach a sleek black car.

He opens the passenger door, and I get in.

Wrong. So wrong.

I give him my address like he asks as he gets in on his side and starts up the car.

Nothing is said between us as he drives to my place.

And once we're there, a confrontation ten years in the making smashes open old wounds I never thought I'd need to deal with again.

"Nice place," Zachary says, walking around the apartment as if he owns it, and gives a low whistle of appreciation. "You sure do enjoy the finer things in life, don't you?"

We've only been here a few moments, but I'm already dreading the conversation his statement will lead to. I'm not sure what I can say that won't make him angrier, so I stay silent, standing by the entryway with my arms crossed over my chest.

He stops in front of the windows, looking out at the lake which graces the view, and spreads his arms wide until one palm lays on either side of the frame.

All I'm able to think as I look at him is how magnificent he is.

And hard.

It is evident life hasn't been kind to him over the years, something I'm sure started with me and our relationship.

He's angry, and he has every right to be. I won't deny what we both know.

I'm just not sure what he wants with me, why he won't just pretend we hadn't seen each other, and simply walk away.

He stands there, silent and guarded, making me more anxious as time passes.

I look down at my watch and see it's only three hours before my fiancé gets home. I don't want to explain Zachary; I've never had to, and I don't plan to start now.

I'm about to take a step forward when he turns to face me and speaks.

"You destroyed my life." The words have some fire in them, but not his face, which is only tired as he stares at me with disgust. "I warned you what would happen if I did anything my parents didn't like before I turned eighteen. I had six months to go when they found out, and they would never have let me shirk my responsibilities toward you, but you just couldn't give me the chance to take care of us, could you?"

"I was sixteen," I say as gently as possible, hating the pain radiating from his voice and his stance. "I never meant to hurt you."

"You took the easy way out," he shouts, swiping an angry hand through the air to make it clear he doesn't want to hear my excuses or reasons. "You got an abortion, you took away my choices, and you know what they did? They fucking sent me away to military school. And once I was there, I had to stay there because unlike you, I had no money. No family to hang onto. No anything. They wouldn't let me come back home even after I graduated. You fucked me over."

There's no point in me yelling back. I merely shake my head as I say, "It wasn't easy for me."

He goes on as if I hadn't even spoken. "I would've done anything to take care of you and our child. But you just couldn't deal, could you? They threatened to cut you off, to leave you as poor as I was, and the idea alone sent you running to do as they told you to. I was good enough to fuck for the lying little rich girl, but not good enough to have a family with. That's what I learned." He waves a hand in the air to indicate the room around him, his sudden laughter not filled with humor at all, but derisive sarcasm. "Was this all worth it?"

"It's not mine." When he quirks a brow and smirks, I clarify. "I...this is where I live with my fiancé. I...my parents cut me off anyway when I hit eighteen."

"Good," he spits out, not even blinking at the

mention of my fiancé as he stalks forward until I'm backed against a door, grabbing my arms and locking them above my head as he repeats himself. "Was it worth it?"

I can't even meet his eyes, staring at his chest which is heaving with his angry breathing, and I shake my head at how much crap I've dealt with over the last ten years. "No. No, it wasn't. If I had known—"

The rest of my words are cut off as his free hand comes up to my chin and forces me to look up at him, followed a second later by his mouth descending on mine. With a little pressure, he shoves his tongue into my mouth, making me whimper at the instant pleasure it sends throughout my body. His hand drops to my side, gliding down as he continues to assault my mouth, and my brain starts screaming the moment his fingertips reach the edge of my skirt.

Wrong as his hand makes quick work of lifting my skirt all around until I'm bared to the surrounding air.

More wrong as the same hand lifts my legs so they are around his hips, before he slips it between my legs and beneath my panties to touch me.

As he slides one finger, then another inside my pussy, he groans into my mouth, and I reciprocate with a moan of my own.

I hate myself for not pulling my mouth away and telling him to stop, which I am easily able to do. I hate myself as he curls his fingers into my g-spot and I buck into his hand, wanting him to do it faster, harder.

He manipulates me with his touch, the fingers on the inside working their magic as his thumb plays with my clit, and I loathe him even more when his expertise has me coming so hard and fast I scream into his mouth.

My mind is blank, my body shuddering with the power of my orgasm. I vaguely register him freeing his cock from his pants, and it's only when he's poised to enter me that he rips his mouth away and says against my lips, "You got exactly what you deserved when they cut you off. I hope you suffered as much as I did. I loved you, and you threw it in my face. I don't love you anymore, but I do want to fuck you, just one last time. I'm going to use you and throw you away just like you did to me. Maybe then it won't fucking hurt anymore."

Tears slip from my eyes as he releases my wrists, commanding harshly, "Keep them right fucking there. I don't want you touching me."

Gripping my ass in his hands, he thrusts up and into me so hard my back slams against the door, and I bite down on my lip to keep from crying out. He pulls to the edge and plunges back in, over and over, relentless as he rubs against me just right, making me orgasm again.

"Fuck yes," he says on a groan as my body trembles around him, his face dropping to my shoulder where he bites me, sinking his teeth in enough to make it sting and no doubt leave a mark.

My arms tire to the point I can't hold them up anymore, and as he drives into me again my hands drop to his shoulders. He freezes and tenses up, still deep inside me, his breathing rough and guttural.

"I'm sorry," I whisper, apologizing for touching him and everything else, the tears coming faster now. "I'm so sorry."

He moves, pulling to the edge before thrusting hard enough my back slams against the door as he says, "I bet you never think about what our lives might've been like, but I do."

I want to tell him he's wrong because he is, but I know he doesn't care what I have to say or what I think. This is about him, not about me, even as he plays my body as if he remembers every inch of it. Even if for all he's rough, his hold is still gentle, an underlying tenderness beneath his words giving away the fact he cares way more than he wants to.

Way more than I ever thought he would after my decision.

He pumps hard and fast, and my nails dig into his shoulders through his shirt as tears stream down my cheeks. Just when I'm about to yell stop because I can't take it anymore, he pauses with a low groan for just an instant before pulling out. I feel his cum splash hot between my legs as he pins me hard to the wall, saying roughly, "Don't want to give you a reason to do what you did before."

His insult is the last straw.

Before he can move away, I lift a hand and slap him across the face, a red mark instantly bursting to life on his cheek as I hiss at him. "Fuck you."

He drops me as he steps away. I hit the floor, yelping from the sudden contact while he shoves his dick back into his pants and snarls, "No, Darcy. Fuck you. Because no matter what might've happened between us if you had kept the baby, anything — fucking *anything* — would've been better than this."

Staring up at him from the floor, I hear the crack in his voice, but before I can react, he steps forward and hauls me off the floor. Then, without another word or glance at me, he turns to the side, sets me on my feet, and storms out the door, slamming it behind him.

It's all I can manage to go to the bathroom and clean up before I climb into my bed and cry myself to sleep.

3

ZACHARY

"You're an asshole."

"So you keep telling me," I retort in a tired voice, having barely stepped inside the house when Erica starts running her mouth. "What did I do this time?"

"It's not what you did," she says with an exaggerated roll of her dark brown eyes and a toss of her equally dark brown hair before glaring at me. "It's all the things you don't do."

"Sign the divorce papers." Pointing to the envelope on the table, I shrug at her and release a forceful, exhausted sigh. "Then what I do and don't do won't bother you so much anymore."

"No!" She steps close and pokes me in the chest with one perfectly manicured fingernail. "They're unfair, and you know it. You want me to walk away with almost nothing."

"Keep your damn hands off me," I snarl, snatching her finger in my hand and flicking it away, hard enough she stumbles a bit before righting her body. "You haven't done anything this whole marriage except bitch and spend all the money I was dumb enough to give you access to. I don't owe you shit, and you've got more than enough money of your own."

Erica continues to look daggers at me with her hands on her hips. "And our daughter? You think you're the one to have full custody of her?"

Straightening my back, my scowl matches hers at the mention of the child I love more than anything else, including my life. "She's *mine*. We both know you got pregnant against my explicit fucking wishes, something you knew I didn't want since before we got married, all because I took you at your word that you were taking your pills. You didn't want her, you wanted to lock me to you, but that's not gonna work. You aren't a mom to her, and we both know it, so I'm keeping her."

"You're the one who didn't want children!"

"No!" The word is a roar, a warning as I shove an angry hand through my hair. "I wanted a child who was planned dand desired by my partner and me at the same fucking time. We started having problems, and you just went on and got pregnant without my consent." She goes to open her mouth and I point my finger at her with pure fury. "The fucking moment I knew about your pregnancy, yeah, I was pissed, but I loved our child every minute since. You thought it would keep us together, though, and it won't. I don't want to be with someone who would be that devious and you've been fighting me for a fucking year now."

Stalking over to the table, I pick up the papers and a pen, slamming them down again in front of her on the counter. "Fucking sign them and get the hell out, or we'll go to court, and you'll get nothing."

"You don't know—"

"Yeah, I damned well do know." Lifting the pen and holding it out to her with an expectant look, my mouth's in a grim line as I modify my tone to something a bit nicer. "Sign so this hell is over, Erica. Stop fighting me. Please."

Watching the woman I married the day after my twenty-first birthday, the indecision evident on her face. We never should've gotten married as I hadn't loved her at all during our time together. But, I had been sick of being alone, and she had been my friend for two years before I asked her out on a date. Within a year of that first date, we were married, and for the first time since Darcy's betrayal, I had trusted a woman enough to let my guard down.

Big mistake.

When we started having trouble, she stopped taking her pills thinking a baby would fix everything, and now a little two-and-a-half-year-old girl named Rose is in the middle of it all.

I put in the effort after our daughter's birth, but I just don't trust Erica anymore, and since I don't love her either, I believe we both deserve better. She isn't taking my little girl from me, though; she's what keeps me going most of the time.

As I stare at Erica in complete silence, she finally breaks, tears trickling down her cheeks as she steps forward and takes the pen from my hand. She signs page after page while I watch, occasionally swiping at her face to get rid of the tears, and once done she sets the pen down with a hard tap.

Then, standing up straight, she squares her shoulders and glares at me while saying in a small voice, "I'll be out by the end of the evening if that's okay with you."

"Of course." As she goes to walk away from the table, I softly add, "Thank you."

She stops and glances over at me with a sad smile. "I know I've angered you, but I didn't think you were serious about this. Whatever, though. You win. No more fighting from me. I just want to keep things civil for our daughter's sake."

I acknowledge her statement with a nod while gathering up the papers. "Absolutely."

After staring at me for another moment, she lets out a heavy sigh and leaves the room. Taking the papers and heading upstairs, I drop them off on my desk inside my home office, and then head to get a quick shower before my daughter returns with the nanny.

Moments later, while standing under the pounding hot water, a tiny bit of shame at how I treated Darcy makes me want to go back over and apologize. Not only for the way I acted but because she no doubt thinks I'm a cheating dirtbag. And to blatantly ignore the fact she said she has a fiancé? I'm an asshole and know it.

She'd been into it, though, and she hadn't stopped me. I would've if she'd said something, but fuck, I'd just wanted to be close to her. The moment I saw her face, my heart started pounding, and even now it continues to beat hard and fast as it hasn't in years.

Not to mention she's even more beautiful than she'd been at sixteen. God, being inside her felt so fucking amazing. And damn, how badly I want to fuck her again, a fact which pisses me off because getting close to her was insane.

I should've walked away the moment I knew who she was, but the look in her eyes gave me pause. The softness mixed with the guilt and pain had made me want to know why, even though a small part of me was thrilled her life hurt as much mine has for so long.

I might've been young ten years ago, but I hadn't been stupid. We'd been friends for years, something neither of our parents liked even though they tolerated it, until one day everything changed.

Isn't that how it always goes?

I shut off the shower and step out, drying off while reminiscing about the first time I kissed her, setting in motion our transition from friends to more.

I had been sixteen and she, fifteen. We were both at a New Year's Eve party, supposed to be supervised by our friend's parents, but they hadn't actually paid attention. All twenty kids had been in the basement, drinking soda, eating a bunch of junk food, and basically just socializing. I hadn't been invited, but Darcy had, and she brought me with her even though her friends didn't like me and never had.

That night, though, no one said anything, and everyone had even been kind to him. Little did I know at the time she told her friends she wanted to date me, and they better start being nicer to him for her sake. In her group, she was the queen, and I can't say becoming part of the popular crowd because of her had been a bad thing because it hadn't been. Nobody fucked with me after that night, and he had always been grateful for that simple fact.

And the kiss which started it all, fuck. Even after all this time, with tonight as a refresher, our first kiss is clear in my mind. I'd been with one girl before Darcy, but that girl nor the women I'd been with since came close to how things were with her. She was my first love.

Dancing that night in their own little corner of the room, she'd wrapped her arms around my neck soft and sweet during a slow dance with a little giggle. Resting her head on my chest, we'd swayed back and forth until she'd suddenly stood on her tiptoes.

"I like you," she'd whispered into my ear before pecking me quickly on the neck and hiding her beautifully freckled face in the crook of my shoulder as if the admission embarrassed her.

I had laughed softly, hugging her closer, appreciating her warmth and the light scent of the lavender and lily perfume I bought her for Christmas days before. "I know."

"No." She had shaken her head, not moving from her position even as she continued with, "I *like* like you, Zach."

My body had reacted instantly to her words,

and for the first time since we'd met, I hadn't had to hide how attractive I found her. However, the way she felt was unexpected, and she lifted her head as I had pulled back to stare down at her with my mouth agape.

But like the forward, get everything she wants girl she was, Darcy had smiled bright and happy while looking up at me. "Kiss me before I start thinking you don't want me like I want you."

As if she planned it with perfect timing, the lights went off right then, the kids counting down loud and clear as midnight approached. But I hadn't waited until the clock struck midnight. I held her close, slid one hand to cup the back of her neck, and locked my lips tightly on hers.

The touch of her lips against mine had sent thrills of pleasure through me, and when she opened her mouth to let me in, I'd followed without question. It hadn't lasted forever, but long enough we kissed right through the New Year arriving, and when we finally parted at the hoots and hollers around us, we hadn't stopped smiling for the rest of the evening.

Really, for the next year, everything had seemed so perfect until it wasn't.

Scowling at the thought, I hang up my towel after drying my hair, and get dressed. Moments later I open the bathroom door to find Erica passing by with her luggage.

She stops, tossing me a tired glance over her shoulder as she says, "That's the last of it. I'll call you later."

I would ask why she isn't waiting for Rose to get back with the nanny so she can say goodbye, but as we both know, she's never been much of a mother. She loves our daughter, but spending time with her isn't something she's ever really done. Rose doesn't even call her 'mommy' which in this matter I'm glad for as it will likely be less traumatic when Erica doesn't see her much.

"All right."

She walks away without another word, and I head to my office to wait on Rose to return.

And when the doorbell rings a half hour later, nothing is more surprising than finding Darcy standing on the doorstep glaring at me.

Fuck.

4

DARCY

"What do you mean you're leaving?"

My fiancé stares at me as I move around the room, gathering my things to pack in my luggage which is open on the bed and already halfway full.

I stop at the obvious distress in his voice and focus on him, one brow lifted in confusion as I cross my arms over my chest. "Did you not just hear what I said a few minutes ago?"

"Of course, I heard you," Oliver says with a huff, sitting on the edge of the bed and putting his black-haired head in his hands. "I'm just not sure I understand why that means you have to leave, Darcy."

If it weren't for the fact we've been together five years now and I know him like nobody else, I would think he's joking right now. But he isn't. I could probably tell him I prostitute myself when he isn't around, and he'd still want to marry me. He's just happy I'm with him, no matter how that happens or what I do otherwise.

"Because after that, there's just no way I can marry you." I sit next to him and touch his upper arm with my hand gently while letting out a shuddering sigh. "The moment I saw him again... everything changed."

Oliver nods, not saying anything else as he keeps his head in his hands, and I stand back up to finish packing.

I told him everything of course. First who Zach was, and then about what happened from the moment I saw him in the store, to when we were in the bathroom, and how we ended up here at the apartment. I've never lied to him; I learned a long time ago how damaging lies could be. Even though Zach called me a liar earlier, I wasn't one now.

All I'd been trying to do in the store bathroom was avoid the exact confrontation we'd ended up having.

There's no going back to my comfortable life with Oliver, in our nearly passionless relationship; not with Zach being so close.

His anger and his touch awakened a part of me

I long thought asleep, and there's no way I'm letting him get away without saying my piece. After my nap earlier, I got onto the computer and found his address, which is where I'm heading once I'm done here with Oliver.

Shit has hit the fan in my life and now it's about to hit it in his.

He thinks he can just say whatever he wants, fuck me like he hates me and misses me all at once, and then just walk out on me. No way, and he's about to learn I'm not the girl I used to be.

I won't take the easy path this time; I won't just pretend earlier never happened. I won't ignore the fact I hurt him in my own naive pursuit of comfort and happiness, but he's not going to treat me like dirt forever because of it. I've paid the price for my decision already, and I'm not willing to pay for it again.

"Where will you go?" Oliver's voice is soft and filled with concern as I put the last of my things inside the luggage and zip it up. I can also hear the roughness in his tone, indicating how hard he's fighting his emotions, and he pulls me into a hug as I sit down next to him once more where he says, "Please don't go. We both know you don't have anywhere to go."

It's true. I've never been good at making

friends, at least not since I was in high school, and Oliver has been my only one for eight years now. Our relationship isn't healthy, and I know it. We're co-dependent on one another, and it's always been a problem. Which we've both ignored, of course, because we've been each other's life.

"I won't abandon you," I say to him, lifting a hand and stroking his hair as he holds me tight against him while I try to ease his anxieties. "You need me, you call me, okay?"

"Same to you." His voice is muffled in my shirt. "Don't make me worry."

"I won't."

We sit like that for a little while, and once he's calmed down enough, I call for a taxi since I don't have a car while he takes my stuff down to the front entryway of the building.

Grabbing my purse, I give one final look at the apartment I've lived in with Oliver for half a decade, and then head downstairs, stepping outside as the taxi pulls up. And as the driver gets out to put my stuff in the truck, Oliver takes me into his arms and presses one final, awkward-as-always kiss to my lips.

"I'll miss you," he whispers as he lets me go just as quick, stepping back and sliding his hands into his pockets, the look in his brown eyes reminding me of a forlorn puppy. "Just remember my door is always open."

With a nod I say, "I'll miss you, too," and get in the taxi, tossing him a final wave as it drives away from the curb after I give the driver the address.

Sitting back, I examine the fact it's insane to go to Zachary's house, because well...he's fucking married. I'm not sure what my plan is exactly. I just show up and announce what? How her husband fucked me and I let him? How we used to date, and I went against what he wanted for my own personal gain, so the sex was really just his anger, disbelief, and utter desire to fuck me once he saw me again?

I don't even know why I'm going there. Or what I want. Not sure if I want a repeat of earlier, which left me with aching thighs and an arousal that springs to instant life when I think about how hard and fast he fucked me, or if I want to slap him across the face again after I tell his wife he cheated on her.

My whole body jerks, jumping as the driver says, "Hey lady, we've arrived. You getting out or what?"

"Sorry." Face flushed, I look out the window to discover a beautiful two-story brick house staring back at me, the light by the front door shining brightly at me. I make sure Zachary's car is in the driveway — which it is — before I say, "Got lost in thought."

The man mutters something as he opens his door and gets out, walking around to take my things out of the trunk as I exit the vehicle as well. Once they are on the curb, I hand him a fifty with a smile and say, "Keep the change."

He looks at the bill, back up at me with his dark brown eyes widening in surprise at the blatant overpayment, and after a moment he nods toward the house. "You want me to wait?"

"Nope, but thanks for asking."

Taking my luggage in hand, I turn toward the house as the driver tosses me one final nervous glance before getting back in the car. I'm still staring at the house as he drives away, and I wonder if I should've come here at all. This is a nice neighborhood, Zachary's place of residence making it clear he's no longer the poor boy I once dated, and I don't miss the irony in this seeing I'm clearly the relatively poor one now. And besides, he made it clear he wanted to use me and throw me away; clearly, me coming to his house was not something he had in mind.

Taking a few deep breaths, I figure I've made it this far so I might as well go all the way, and walk up to the door. Ringing the doorbell once, holding it down for a few seconds for extra effect,

I let a whole minute pass before I decide to ring it again.

But before I can do that, the door swings open, and there stands Zachary without a shirt on. My eyes instantly fall to his bare chest, the v and light dusting of hair leading straight down to the rim of his jeans, where they hang low on his hips and make you wonder what's beneath. Well, if you had to wonder, which I don't as I'm obviously intimately acquainted with his equipment.

"What are you doing here?"

His snarled words have me lifting my head and locking my eyes on his, my mouth turning down in a scowl to match his irritable tone, all while the spicy smell of whatever cologne he's put on teases my senses.

But if he's gonna be an ass then so am I. "I don't know. Why do you smell like a cheap hooker?"

His hot gaze does a once-over down my body, the corner of his lip quirking up as he replies, "Maybe I fucked one earlier. You tell me."

"Oh yeah," I shoot back, letting go of the handle on my luggage to curl my hands into fists at my sides. "About that. You owe me a grand for the quickie. You ran out so fast I didn't get a chance to give you my pricing."

He laughs, the sound rich, deep, and doing things to my insides I don't even want to admit to. I hate him for being able to insult me and then turn me on with the sound of his amusement. To make it worse, he continues to chuckle as he reaches into his pocket, jiggles it a time or two before bringing his hand back out, and shows me two quarters in the palm of his hand.

"All I've got is fifty-cents, so you better take it before I change my mind and keep it."

Before I even think better of it, or he has a chance to react, my arm lifts and I punch him square in the stomach. He sucks in a shocked breath, his eyes widening as one of his hands comes up to touch where I hit him while I instantly cradle my fist in my other hand with a gasp of my own. Both sounds mix with the pings of the quarters as they fall from his hand and land on the stone of his steps, and when he finally manages to speak, he simply says, "Fuck."

The fact he hadn't seen it coming means I hurt him before he could tighten up his abs, but the sting of my hand compared to a little hiss of surprise from him says the pain affects me more. I hold my hand against my chest, wondering if I've sprained it, while he glares at me once more as he straightens up.

"I suppose you want to come inside."

"Yep." He steps back quick as I stride past him into the house, continuing to cradle my hurting hand as I say, "Since you're the one who got me into this mess, now you get to put up with me until I find a place of my own." Stopping, I turn around and glare at him as he simply stands there, watching me with an indiscernible look on his face. "Grab my bags too, why don't you?"

Turning around without replying, he brings my luggage inside and sets it right next to the door before shutting it. After, he walks toward and then past me, forcing me to follow him. He leads us down the hallway and into the kitchen, where he opens the fridge and while looking inside asks, "Drink?"

"No," I reply while rolling my eyes at his back. "Some ice for my hand would be nice."

Pulling out a beer bottle, he closes the door and leans against the fridge while twisting off the cap, taking a swig while staring at me with his lips tipped up at the edges. "Would you now? Is that truly necessary, with you being you and all?"

Obviously missing his meaning, I frown at him. "Huh?"

For some reason, this amuses him, and the small quirk of his lips becomes a full-fledged grin as he shrugs. "Cold heart, no soul. What do you need ice for? Your hand'll be okay in no time considering you're one big ice block yourself."

Apparently he desires for me to hit him again,

but it's his lucky day because my hand hurts enough already.

"Wow." Glaring at him, I flip him off with my non-injured hand before walking over to the sink and turning on the cold water, shoving the other under it while flexing and moving it around a bit to keep it from stiffening up. "You're an asshole, Zach."

His reply is pure sarcasm. "Ouch. I've never heard that before." He pauses, takes a drink as I continue to glare at him while the water rushes over my hand, and then shakes his head, his face growing serious. "You can't stay here."

"Oh?" I turn off the water and grab a close by hand towel to dry off my hand, which still aches but not as badly, lifting a brow at him in question while asking him the obvious. "Why not? Because of your wife? Don't you think she should know what you did earlier?"

"What I did?" He laughs, finishing his beer and putting the bottle on the counter, before sliding his hands into his pockets casually as he continues to stare at me intently. "You were a willing participant."

"Would I be standing here otherwise?"

Running a hand through his short hair, he sighs and stands up straight. "My soon-to-be ex-wife no longer lives here, Darcy, but that's not why you can't stay."

His statement has me blinking a few times in confusion although I'm relieved he isn't cheater and a total asshole, just ninety-nine percent. "So, earlier...?"

"I was fucking with you." He lifts his shoulders, the smile still on his face, as he walks closer and stops right in front of where I'm standing. "I've been trying to get her to sign the papers for a year. She finally did today not too long ago, took her stuff, and left."

My body responds with desire at his closeness and my mind screams for me to get away from this man who does nothing but hate me with his mouth while wanting me with his body. When I try to step away, he blocks me in against the counter, placing a hand on either side of its edge while looking down at me with barely concealed intent.

"Don't," I whisper while placing a hand flat against his chest to punctuate my statement. "We shouldn't—"

He cuts me off with fast and hot kiss along with one of his hands dropping down to cup an ass cheek in his palm, giving it a hard squeeze as he grinds his lower body against mine, making it clear with his rock-hard arousal how much he wants me, as if I had any doubts.

His tongue invades my mouth, my tongue battling his for dominance in a fight it's quickly losing, and his hand slides down my ass and in-between my legs from behind. Instinctively wiggling, he chuckles into my mouth, taking my wiggling for encouragement as his hand goes underneath my skirt, skimming the silky fabric of my panties until he's cupping me between the legs. I expect him to move them out of his way and slip a finger inside me, but he doesn't.

Instead, he goes still, and when an involuntary whimper falls from my lips, he drags his mouth away from mine, his reluctance apparent as he murmurs against my mouth, "You need to leave. Now."

Yes, I do. Well, I should, but the way he's holding me tells me what he wants doesn't match what he's telling me, so I ask him the obvious question. "Why can't I stay?"

But he doesn't get to answer me, removing his hand and jumping away as the door in the kitchen opens, making me turn away in embarrassment while smoothing my skirt down to make sure everything is in place while wondering who would just walk into Zach's house if his wife left like he said.

I'm not prepared for the little girl with blonde pigtails who runs in.

Or for her to slam into Zachary's leg, wrap her arms around his legs as she looks up into his face, and squeals happily, "Daddy!"

The thunderous expression on his face as he glances at me while picking his daughter up indicates he isn't too pleased with her returning home before I left either. Especially when she encircles his neck with her arms, pecks him on the cheek, then turns her face until she's looking right at me with her beautiful blue eyes and says in a sweet voice, "Hey-yo."

Before I can respond, a short, dark-haired woman walks in the door and says in a raised voice, "So sorry, Mister Haider! She saw you were home and took off for the door before I could stop her and—"

Cutting off as she spots me, she stops walking at the same time Zach turns toward her and lowers the little girl back to the floor, shaking his head. "No worries, Tara. You may have the rest of the evening off."

"Oh." Tara looks confused, her eyes darting from him to me and back again. "I thought I watched Rose until—"

Zach doesn't let her finish speaking, his tone growing harsh and short while Tara barely holds back her wince at the bite of his words. "My plans for the evening have changed. We'll see you in the morning."

"Okay. See you then."

When she turns and leaves, I expect him to say something to me, but instead, he walks out of the kitchen without even looking at me, leaving me to wonder what to do next and shocked as hell that he's a father.

5

ZACHARY

Shit.

The last thing I need is for Darcy to stay at my place. Not only because of our past, but also because of our distinct issues here in the present and how much I desire to repeat our interlude from earlier over and over again until we're both too exhausted to speak.

That wouldn't be much of a problem if it weren't for the fact her little appearance on my doorstep — and our subsequent jabbing at each other — hadn't lifted her up in my esteem just a notch more than earlier today had.

She's changed, which shouldn't surprise me after all these years because for most people change is inevitable, yet it does. And she can hold her own against me, which is dangerous all on its own, making me itch to put her over my lap and punish her for everything she put me through.

Now, Rose is sound asleep in her bedroom and Darcy sits in the living room on the couch a few inches from where I stand, a nervous smile gracing her lips as she watches me. Her hands rub together in her lap, and her tongue darts out every so often to wet her lips; she's waiting for me to speak first.

The problem is, I don't know what to say. How can I put into words everything I'm thinking and feeling after all these years along with the day we've both had?

Why had I let her in earlier? Or allowed her to stay after telling her to leave in the kitchen earlier right before Rose bolted in?

All I know is she can't remain here in my home. It isn't good for my daughter and will be even worse for me. I screwed up with my actions toward Darcy earlier today; I hadn't expected my past to rear its head as it had, but I'll be damned if she comes in to fuck things up for me when I'm finally getting my head on straight.

Especially after I've finally managed to get Erica to agree to stop fighting me on the divorce so we can both move on with our lives.

Taking a seat in the chair, I clasp my hands together and lean forward, waiting for her to meet my gaze before saying, "It's late. You can stay the night, but you'll need to leave before Rose rises in the morning."

She blinks, biting her lip as she sits back and crosses her arms over her chest, the movement lifting her breasts a little. The curve of her lips firm as she breaks my hold on her gaze, glancing around the room for a brief moment before looking back at me and changing the topic. "This house is lovely."

"It is."

"And different from the others around it. Usually, houses in these sorts of neighborhoods look similar."

If I weren't exhausted, I would find the energy to summon a smile at her keen observation and tell her what she's already deduced, that it was custom designed by me. "They do."

She stares for a moment and then smiles. "I would like a drink."

"Water from the tap is that way." I point at the kitchen, stand up at her frown and clear my throat. "I'm heading to bed. I trust you can find the way back to your room."

"Yes, I can, but—" She rises and smooths her skirt, her eyes flicking to the floor before she lifts her gaze back to mine. "I thought we would talk for a bit. I mean, it's been a long time and..."

Unsure of what to say as she drifts off, her hopeful expression makes me feel like an ass because I'm trying to avoid her company and she knows, so I maintain the distance with my next question. "Why are you here, Darcy? Does your fiancé know you're here?"

"I told you."

"No. You said you were going to stay here until you found a place of your own."

She frowns, her face clearing after a second as she shrugs. "Okay. Well, we aren't together anymore, and I've got nowhere to go. And after earlier..."

Shit. I'm partly to blame for this, which means if I kick her out come tomorrow morning, I'm an even bigger asshole than usual. Muttering, I sit back down in the chair. "Wonderful."

"Clearly, I had no idea about your daughter and I...I don't want to put you out." She smiles nervously when I flick my gaze to hers as she stands in front of me rubbing her hands together. "A week or two, maybe three tops, before I'll have the money to get my own place. Oliver would've let me stay with him, he's a good man, but I just...couldn't. Not anymore."

I study her face, yet she doesn't look upset over the loss of the relationship, which peaks my interest against my better judgment. She found my address, came to my house, and now wants to stay for as long as three weeks all because this morning I didn't walk the hell away from her.

And there's nothing I want less than for this woman to stay with me for a moment longer than she has to.

"Sit down," I tell her while standing again. "I'll get us drinks, and we'll talk for a little while, see if we can find a solution that suits us both."

"Okay," she says, taking a seat on the couch as I walk past her and out of the room.

When I return with two beers, she accepts the one I hand her and twists off the top, sipping as I sit so we're facing one another. "Did you have something specific you wanted to talk about, Darcy?"

"Yes. We should discuss all the things you said and all the replies you didn't get to hear."

"Is that necessary?"

"You were pretty nasty." She raises her hand, palm out, to stop me when I start to say something. "I understand why and you had every right to be angry with me, but I...I didn't make that decision lightly. No matter what, I never wanted to hurt you."

There isn't much to say in response that won't bring up past pain and drudge up old wounds on my end, and for her, I can only guess how the choice she made affected her life. However, her sincerity is plain to see, and it deserves my recognition. "It doesn't change what happened, but I believe your intentions were your own and had nothing to do with me."

Which, of course, had been the whole problem. She hadn't considered my feelings or desires, at all.

With a sigh, she finishes her beer and sets the empty bottle on the table. "My parents were awful, all right? Beyond anything everyone knew about them, they were terrible people who would've turned our lives — and that of their grandchild — into a living hell. I would've been seventeen by the birth, but the idea of being stuck with them even for a year more along with a baby was more than I could handle."

"You wouldn't have had to live with them. I told you I would take care of us."

She shakes her head and scoffs. "You thought everything was going to be okay, but I didn't. I grew up with every aspect of my life being taken care of for me. I didn't even know how to cook or do laundry. I couldn't even take care of myself, so I knew there wasn't a good chance of me taking care of a baby and going to school and everything else, even with your help. I would've needed them, and I didn't want to fucking need them in my life like that."

"You think I don't know the reasons for your

choice, for doing the opposite of what I wanted for us?"

"No, how would I when you threw about how it was money in my face?" When I don't reply, merely lifting a brow to indicate we both understand I have my reasons, she flashes me a tight smile. "Sure, I cared about money, but it's a fact money is necessary to survive, especially with a baby. It wasn't, however, the only or even the main reason for my decision."

"There's no point in discussing this. I won't ever believe that what you did was the right course of action to take; not now when I have a child and can't imagine my life without her."

She stands up, clenching her fists at her sides and glaring at me. "You said anything would've been better than what I did, but you have no way to know that. You think I didn't wonder what might've happened, especially after it tore us apart and you were gone from my life? I loved you. And you hated me for making the right choice for myself after swearing you would love me always, no matter what. But you didn't mean it. Your love had conditions, just as it did with my parents, and in the end, I ended up with nothing. It wasn't something I deserved for making the best decision that could be made under the circumstances."

With that, she whirls around and stomps off

before I can even process what she's said, let alone formulate an appropriate reply.

And I don't follow her because the last thing either of us needs is to make an already complicated situation worse.

Instead, I turn off the lights and head up to bed since Rose is an early riser, thinking about what Darcy said even though I don't want to and wondering what will happen come morning since our conversation hadn't resolved anything.

6

DARCY

"I'll be gone after I'm finished eating," I say, stabbing some scrambled eggs onto my fork as Zachary walks into the kitchen at seven the next morning and casts a glance toward me while heading to the fridge. "Hope that's soon enough for you."

I watch as he opens the fridge, grabs the orange juice, and shuts the door before walking over to a cupboard. Taking out a glass, he ignores my comment while pouring, and places it back in the fridge. Then, he turns to me, takes a drink of his juice, and says, "Did you sleep well?"

"As much as one can sleep when they're faced with being turned out in the morning." My answer is a little disingenuous — he hadn't invited me here, after all — but after last night, I don't think it matters much at all to him as long as I leave. "These eggs are good, however."

"Local," he tells me with a smile, ignoring the first part of what I said. "Better than store bought ones."

His random remark amuses me, however, and I have to squash down a smile. "Can't say I've ever entertained the thought that there would be a difference."

"Most people don't."

"Well, that's great." Eating the last of my eggs, I stand up, take the plate over to the sink, and rinse it before turning to face him. "Thanks for letting me stay the night."

The kitchen door opens as he opens his mouth to reply and the woman, Tara, from yesterday steps inside. Zach walks past me, grabs her arm, and pulls her into the other room while speaking in a tone low enough I can't hear what he says.

Reaching into my pocket, I pull out my phone and lean against the sink, scrolling through my Facebook news feed as I do every morning. I don't exactly have many friends, so it's mainly filled with my co-workers, and of course, Oliver. I stop at his post from last night shortly after I left, where it only says he's "feeling sad."

As I haven't even talked to him since leaving

yesterday, I tap the messages icon on my phone to send him a text. *"Hey. Everything okay?"*

Then, I press the power button to turn the screen off and shove the phone back into my pocket. I don't expect him to answer for a while since he'll be on his way to work now if he hasn't called in sick, which he might've done after me leaving yesterday; emotional things tend to make him so upset he gets migraines after.

Only my phone buzzes not long after and I tug it back out to read the reply from Oliver. *"No. Not feeling well so at home."*

Not sure what to say, I keep it simple. *"I'm sorry. I hope you feel better soon."*

"I will when you come back. You know I hate living alone."

Yeah, I do, because I'm the same way. That's basically how we came to live with each other in the first place. From dorms to a place together upon graduation so neither of us was alone and he gladly paid most of the bills for the privilege. So his text makes me feel like a jerk because I've no doubt he didn't get much sleep last night, if at all.

Not that I did either after my little parting shot at Zach and the understanding he isn't going to let me stay here with him, which means I will have to go back to living with Oliver because I just can't afford a place of my own with what I make. Well, unless I want to answer an ad for a roommate and live with a total stranger, which I don't, because living with someone I have no previous acquaintance with makes me want to barf.

Hell, just having that thought makes my chest squeeze painfully with anxiety and immense panic.

Yep. I'm genuinely stuck in a hell of my own making, and I guess I'm lucky that Oliver will let me come back after yesterday. What the hell had I been thinking?

Even with the way Zach kissed me yesterday in the kitchen and the sex before that, I shouldn't have been so rash. Ten years ago, I unapologetically and explicitly went against his wishes, and he's hated my guts since.

Despite the crazy attraction remaining between us, I can't fucking blame him for not forgiving me.

He doesn't want me here and he most certainly doesn't want me around his daughter. He told me I needed to leave, and after his daughter had shown up, I understood why without him having to say a word, even as I hoped for the rest of the evening that he would change his mind.

But then our conversation last night...ugh. The pain on his face, in his words, had truly driven everything home.

Things might've been different. We might've had a child. And he can't imagine a life with his daughter, which means when he looks at me, all he sees is the decision I made when I was too young to realize how much it would forever change everything.

It didn't matter that I thought I was doing the right thing at the time; my reasons would never make a difference to him.

So it had been foolish to come here, to show him how much that little moment in time with him had affected me, which means now I need to extricate myself from this situation. I need to go back to the life I've been living because it's the one I've built.

It isn't perfect or ideal, but it's mine.

Using the app on my phone, I hail a cab to my location and walk over to the door, hoping Zach doesn't come back into the kitchen before my phone notifies me about the taxi waiting outside.

I let out a deep breath of relief when he doesn't, grab the handles of my luggage, and exit out of his door and his life as if I had never been here at all.

Shutting the door to the apartment behind me, I put my keys on the table nearby, slip out of my heels, and leave them there along with my luggage before heading to the bedroom.

Oliver doesn't even stir as I open the door and walk in the room, unzipping my dress to slip out of it, and place it on the chair before turning toward the bed in my bra and underwear.

He doesn't startle even when I climb into bed and slide under the blankets. Instead, he merely opens his eyes, smiles while opening his arms, and waits until I'm snuggled in his familiar embrace before murmuring, "I'm so glad you're back."

All I can do is think this is best because, for the last eight years, Oliver has been the only constant in my life, which has to count for more than an angry man with blue eyes and the ability to make me want to have made a different choice.

It has to since the one thing I don't need is to feel unhappy with my life again as I used to for so long. My life is what it is because of the things I've done and having taken responsibility for those actions meant I had finally found peace after not having it for so long.

And I can't let Zach ruin it. Not with his touch, or his memory, or his righteous anger about our destruction at my hands.

No, co-dependent or not, I will do well to remain in the safety of Oliver's unexciting but steady love, rather than hold out for something to happen with a man who has yet to forgive me and may never do so, especially when he had barely been civil to me from the moment we faced one another again.

I remind myself of this while swiping away a traitor tear from my cheek seconds before Oliver gently turns me in his hold and captures my lips with his, taking me back as his without another word said between us on the matter.

WE'VE JUST FINISHED EATING BREAKFAST three days later when Oliver reaches across the table, covers my left hand that once again sports the engagement ring he bought me, and says, "We should finally get married."

Laughing softly, I slide my hand out from under his and grab my plate, rising from my seat to take it over to the sink. He follows with his and stands next to me as I wash the dishes, smiling again when I eventually look at him to remark, "You're serious."

"Yes." After I turn off the water and dry off my hands, he pulls me into his arms and gives me a brief, dry kiss on the lips before murmuring against them, "There's no good reason not to now, is there?"

It's true; there isn't. I chose to come back, climb into the bed we shared, and accept his ring on my finger once more. He hasn't asked about what happened with Zach, and I know it's because he doesn't find it necessary since I came back to him.

He's also been happier than I've ever seen him be during our entire relationship. Combine that with the impossible to ignore fact that I haven't heard from Zach since walking out of his place — even without my phone number, he knows where he can find me — and I'm convinced this decision is right after making a lot of wrong ones.

Zach saw me, paid me back in his own twisted way for the way I made him feel, and hurt me with his insults on top of it. His actions speak for him — both to his feelings and for not wanting me in his life — and I'm not the type of woman to chase anyone, ever.

So I return Oliver's smile, slide my arms up around his neck, and plant a reciprocating kiss on his mouth as I admit, "No, there isn't. Did you have something in mind?"

His entire face lights up with joy as his arms tighten around my waist. "This weekend on our sixth anniversary. It'll be perfect."

It won't be, not really.

I've always imagined a wedding — location unimportant in the big picture — with my father walking me down the aisle after my mother helped me get ready, excited for her only child's new life along with her future grandchildren, and the chairs on each side of the aisle filled with other family as well as lots of friends.

An old desire I still wish for yet will never happen because my parents haven't spoken to me since disinheriting me the day after I turned eighteen. And, once I learned how little real life mirrored the one I grew up in, the few friends I had hadn't lasted past high school either.

He knows all of this, but the fact we won't have the wedding I've dreamt of isn't his fault, so that's why I don't bring it up. He'll do everything to make our wedding romantic, even if it's just the two of us and the justice of the peace, and I won't ruin it by dwelling on everything that will be missing from what should be the happiest moment of my life.

"I can't wait," I finally reply softly, stepping up on my tiptoes to press a slightly warm and longer kiss to his mouth in hopes he doesn't notice the slight sadness in my voice.

He doesn't, ending our embrace a few moments later so we can both finish getting ready for the day, and giving me a glimpse of what the rest of our lives will be like at the same time.

Predictable, but safe, and exactly what I tell myself I need even if it isn't true.

7

ZACHARY

The moment I realized she left my place without saying goodbye, I should've gone after her to explain, but I didn't.

And now, for the last week, I've wanted to kick my own ass for not doing it, except I don't know where she went. She said she couldn't stay with her ex-fiancé anymore, and although that doesn't mean she didn't go back there, I don't want to show up and try to explain myself to the man considering what we'd done if she isn't there.

And maybe she is. They may have gotten back together, and who am I to show up after making it blatantly clear to her that she couldn't stay with me?

So I've left it alone because it's for the best — for both Rose and me — and I've taken the fact I haven't seen her since as confirmation. I don't know how long she's lived here, but I have for almost a decade, and the bookstore had been the only time I ran into her in a public place.

My mother waves at me from her table as Rose and I step into our favorite local food joint, pulling me away from my thoughts about Darcy, and Rose takes off with a squeal toward her grandmother.

Although I told Darcy my parents wouldn't let me come home after they sent me to military school, which was true, she hadn't fucked me over as I said. Well, not really. My parents never stopped speaking to me or guiding me in my life unlike hers. Yes, they'd been angry with me and hadn't wanted me on such a hard path at a young age, but they always loved me and wanted me to succeed.

Her choice had devastated them as much as it had me because I had believed with all my heart that we were having a baby, and had told them what was going on so as to not hide anything. They weren't happy we would have a child in our teens, but would've supported us a hundred percent.

Then, she'd gotten an abortion, and they wanted to prevent another pregnancy from happening, as well as get me away from what they referred to as "the bad influence of *that girl*," so they did something about it.

At the time, their decision hurt because it took me from them, my younger brother and sister, and the place I'd lived all my life. However, after a while, I understand why they made that choice and ended up making a life for myself here. Four years ago, when my younger sister finished high school, they both retired from their jobs and followed her to school out here, where they now live in a house I bought for them thanks to my successful career as an Architect.

I imagine they are like all parents that love their children and don't believe the raising ends when they hit adulthood. The difference is that now they give their opinions because I am their son, and that is their right, yet I am free to make my own decision in spite of it, which I usually do.

They didn't like Erica, but they dote on Rose, which is what matters to me more than anything else now regarding our relationship.

Something tells me they will never think any woman is good enough for me and approval had been evident in my mother's eyes a few weeks ago when I told her dating anyone wasn't on my radar for the foreseeable future, as all my energy will be on work and raising Rose.

And it remains true now, even with what happened with Darcy, which I need to forget about before I do something stupid like track her down to ask why she hadn't waited for me to come back that day before leaving.

"Darling," my mother says as I finally reach the table, Rose already sitting beside her and coloring on the paper for kids provided by the restaurant. She hugs me, then pats the table as she sits again. "How's everything?"

"Pretty good. Work's hectic as always."

She nods and then lifts a brow with a side glance at Rose. "And with her gone?"

"She's fine. Doesn't even notice."

"Good." She gets the attention of a nearby waiter while smiling at me. "A child needs their mother, but only if that mother is going to take care of them. Otherwise, it's best she's gone before she hurts the girl."

"Mother."

I don't have to say more than that, even if I partly agree with her, as she heeds the warning in my voice with a sigh. "Fine. You know my feelings on the matter so I won't speak of it any longer."

She knows her thoughts on the matter isn't what I'm rebuking; it's her discussing it in front of Rose that I don't approve of.

"Thank you." As the waiter approaches, I reach for the water already sitting on the table and change the topic. "How's Dad doing?"

"Oh, you know, he isn't taking it easy like the

doctor said, but when has your father ever listened to anyone's professional advice in his entire life?"

We both laugh because the answer is never and then the waiter arrives to take our orders.

When they're gone, I take a sip of the water and shake my head. "I've told him to take it easy when he calls, but it doesn't seem to make a difference either."

"He's stubborn, and that's what I've been blessed with my entire life. A stubborn husband who gave me three equally obstinate children." Her statement is filled with affection, and she winks at me when I laugh because it's true. "Not that I would have it any other way, of course."

No, she wouldn't, as she can and does give us all a run for our money when it comes to being obstinate.

Rose smacks her crayon down on the table at that exact moment and crosses her arm over her chest with attitude as she looks at me to declare, "Food!"

"It's coming, sweetheart." My mother picks up her water and turns to Rose, holding the glass up to distract her. "Are you thirsty?"

She shakes her head yet reaches for the water anyway. After a few sips, she scrunches her nose and turns back to the paper, picking up her crayon again.

My mother snickers and takes a sip before setting the glass back down. "She reminds me of you at that age. You were always demanding, but it didn't take much to distract you, no matter how upset you were."

"Then I grew up."

"Yes, you made up for that as a teen, but you're doing wonderfully now, and I'm proud of the man you've become."

Just like that, Darcy is back on my mind.

I doubt my mother would be pleased with my treatment of her recently no matter how she felt about her back then. As angry as they'd been, I never heard them say anything about Darcy other than referring to her as a bad influence and commenting on how awful her parents were to manipulate her into making the decision she did.

And even with not wanting her to stay at my house, I should've apologized for my behavior at the bookstore and afterward when she showed up at my place. I was — am — an asshole and deserved more than a punch to the stomach at the insults I threw her way.

She isn't the same girl from ten years ago just like I'm not the same boy and no matter our past, she deserves better from someone who claimed to love her at one point.

I don't say any of this to my mother as our food

arrives, making a promise to myself instead to apologize to Darcy the next time I see her if and when it happens because I don't want to cause either of us any more pain.

Then, perhaps I can put all my focus on my daughter where it belongs instead of my guilt at being the type of man who would treat another person with such disregard no matter how much they've hurt me.

My chance arrives two weeks later while shopping for next week's groceries.

Rose is with my parents for the day — they spend every Saturday together — and one of the benefits to that is being able to shop without her howling for things as we walk through the store.

She's got a sweet tooth, especially for gummy bears, and I have trouble saying no sometimes to her adorable pout, so it's better this way.

Today, for certain, as I round the corner into the aisle containing frozen pizza, and there Darcy stands in front of where the Digiorno's are located.

Heading in her direction, she doesn't realize anyone's approached until I stop right beside her, and her eyes widen when her focus is jerked away from the boxes to me. Instead of saying something, she shoves one of the pizza's back into the freezer, tosses the other in her cart, and takes the handle in a tight grip with both hands while dragging her gaze away to stare at where I just came from.

"Wait," I say, reaching over to grab her cart before she can walk away, and smile when she acknowledges my action with an icy glare. "I don't want to bother you. Just need to apologize for the way I treated you when we saw each other again and later for the insults at my house. It wasn't right, and I'm sorry."

She blinks, then laughs — the sound being one I can only describe as decidedly sarcastic — and points at my hand on her cart with another glare until I remove it. "Now you're sorry? I wanted to know if it was you that day, but you took it further instead of letting me go, bringing all sorts of shit to the surface in the process, and now you want to apologize for it?" She lifts her left hand to shove it through her hair, blows out a harsh breath, and then flicks me off after lowering her arm. "Fuck you, Zach."

Two thoughts hit me at once, but the fact she thinks I'm apologizing for having sex with her is quickly pushed aside by the sight of a fucking wedding band nestled next to the engagement ring on her ring finger.

Snatching her hand, I grasp it tight in mine to

do the most stupid thing I can, which is state the obvious in an incredulous tone. "You married him."

"I did." She yanks her hand from my hold and places it on the cart again with a smirk. "Is there anything else?"

"Why?"

"Because I need to get home—"

I step closer and cut her off with a single shake of my head. "No. You came to my place, said it was over to the point you needed a place to stay, and now you've married him? Why?"

She straightens up and leans in until our faces nearly meet, with the angriest expression I've ever seen on her face as she hisses, "I married him two weeks ago. Why? The better question is, why not? I came to you, you made it clear I wasn't welcome, and I decided the best thing to do was to go back to the life I had; to forget you ever showed back up in it."

I don't need this in my life, not when I need to focus on Rose, yet I can't resist the fire and obvious agony in her eyes. Lifting my right hand, I cup her cheek in my head and watch her anger war with the feelings she doesn't want to have as I murmur, "And how's that going for you? Go on, lie to me if that's what you need to get through the day."

When she doesn't move away, I prepare for all sorts of her response scenarios such as a smack, yet nothing prepares me for the sudden death of the fire in her eyes, only to be replaced with enough ice to kill me were it real.

"You know what I wish?" She whispers while stepping back, my fingers skimming her face until finally they no longer touch her, and our gazes lock as she slaps me with the unexpected vehemence of her words. "Instead of wishing I knew what might've happened between us, now I merely want to have never met you at all, and I ask that you act as that is the truth if or when you feel the urge to approach me again in the future."

Similar to the night at my house, she rushes away without letting me reply and leaves me standing there wondering how the hell my apology had derailed into receiving that from her.

And as I resume shopping a few minutes later, I'm not sure what pisses me off more...the fact I don't know if her words were a lie, or how I'm bothered by the fact she got married.

Either way, there's nothing I can do besides give her exactly what she asked for, and telling myself we never met at all is precisely what I do before continuing on with the rest of my day.

8

Oliver steps into the kitchen after I arrive home and presses a kiss to my bared shoulder before walking over to the grocery bags on the counter. "Did you get everything?"

"Yes. I had to go to a few places to find a few of the items, but it's all there."

"Ah," he said without glancing at me, all his focus on emptying the bags for tonight's important dinner with his boss, which he hopes will finally lead to a much-deserved promotion. "I wondered what was taking longer than usual."

It wasn't locating the groceries that kept me, but I don't say that.

"Well, it's all there," I tell him instead and close my eyes with a sigh before forcing them open. "I'm going to need a nap before this dinner, so if you don't need my help...?"

He makes a dismissive motion with his hand and tosses a smile at me. "Nope, go on. I'll wake you later in time to get ready."

No need to respond as he starts moving around the kitchen, so I head toward the bedroom, pushing down the straps of my sundress while shutting the door with my foot.

The tears I've been holding back since running into Zachary finally make their way out and slide down my cheeks while the ache in my chest builds to an almost unbearable degree.

His sudden appearance in the store caught me off guard.

I shouldn't have said those awful things to him. Yes, he had been apologizing for the terrible things he'd said to me but the look on his face when he realized I married Oliver had made my already shitty morning worse.

Combined with the way he had gripped my hand as if he wanted to rip the rings off, I could've sworn at that moment he was upset at the unexpected news.

For a second, I had enjoyed his apparent jealousy, but only for that brief instant before the reality of my situation made it imperative we both shove aside whatever was between us. And I hadn't known how to make him do that without being mean because when I'm nice for even a moment, we end up close...something we can never be again.

But now, I regret my words, because I don't want to have never met him and would never actually wish for it either. And the part of me that's always wondered about the life I might've had is still there, something that hasn't changed since a few weeks after I made an irrevocable decision.

Especially after my parents made it clear nothing I did would ever earn their forgiveness for my indiscretion with the boy whose name they would never allow to pass their lips — or mine for the rest of the time I remained at home.

To this day, I've yet to forgive *them* for...well, everything, and I doubt I ever will.

Swiping at the tears on my face, I take a deep breath and head into the master bathroom while wearing nothing more than my bra and panties, all while hoping Zach will forgive me one day, at least, for what I put him through.

Then, I make myself stop thinking about him and crouch down to pull out the bag I hid earlier from the cabinet beneath the bathroom sink. Rising, I close the door as quiet as I can and pull the box out from the bag, staring down at the pregnancy test with newfound tears.

I'm a few days late, and that's only ever

happened one time before, so I need to find out in case the stress of not knowing is making my period even later.

Yanking down my panties, I take a seat on the toilet, tear open the box, and rip the foil on the test to take it out. Then, I pee on the stick as instructed, replace the cap, and place it on the counter before finishing up.

The results don't take long.

Two pink, solid lines stare me in the face when I straighten up from tugging my underwear back up and, from this moment on, I know nothing will ever be the same even as my chest begins to prick with panic.

It isn't even the fact I'm going to have a baby. No. It's having spent the last two weeks wondering if I made a mistake in marrying Oliver because I couldn't get Zach off my mind no matter how much I tried.

But then, I woke up feeling sick to my stomach and finally realized my period was late.

And the test confirms that, mistake or not, there's no turning back now because I want this child to grow up with an intact family, where both parents give their all.

For better or worse, this is my life, and I'm facing it head on in a way I should've all those years ago instead of fearing the changes to come.

So I dry my tears, take another deep breath while grabbing the test, and then head to the kitchen to tell Oliver we're going to be parents.

EVERYTHING CHANGES FOR THE BETTER IN mine and Oliver's relationship after discovering we're having a baby.

Two days after dinner with his boss, he came home and took me in his arms, whirling me around with excitement at landing the promotion, and immediately said, "Now to buy a house so we can raise our family outside the city."

I haven't thought about leaving the city since arriving here, but I agreed with his idea, as the lure of having our own house with a yard without the noise of neighbors and cars at all hours of the night was too big to ignore.

So here we stand in one of the most beautiful houses I've ever seen, thirty minutes outside of town, and one look at Oliver's face reveals he likes it as much as I do.

The realtor talks as she guides us through the first floor and then leads us to the second. Oliver holds my hand, squeezing it and winking at me when she says, "Four beds and two baths," at which point he catches her eye and comments, "Sounds perfect for a growing family like ours."

Understanding his meaning, she agrees with a bright smile and begins to talk up all the features more, taking considerable delight in pointing out the two acres of land surrounding the house as we walk back down the steps that land us back in the foyer.

Oliver's phone rings then. He pulls it out of pocket and after glancing at the screen, tosses an apologetic smile at both of us. "I need to take this. I'll be just a moment."

As he walks off toward the kitchen, I grimace at the lady and say, "Sorry."

She shakes her head with a laugh. "Don't worry about it, hon. Happens all the time, usually with the husbands. Now," she says with a quick glimpse around us. "Do you have any questions or anything you want to see again?"

"No, thank you. It's just…" I take a deep breath and indicate the whole house with a wave of my hand. "I would love to live here. This house is stunning."

"Isn't it? The last custom home we have to offer. The architect held onto this one for quite a while but finally allowed us to put it up for sale a few days ago although it was built two years ago."

That's a big gap. "Oh, wow."

"Yes. We all thought he would move in with his family, but I guess now they're getting divorced." She blushes when I lift my eyebrow at her sharing this and turns toward the door, then laughs before clearing her throat. "Speaking of him, he's here now to sign the final papers. If you'll give me a few moments?"

"Sure. I need to sit down anyway." Heading back toward the living room as she nods at me while opening the door, I find one of the comfortable wingback chairs they're using to furnish the house for show and take a seat.

I close my eyes, listening to her soft laughter and the barely audible rumble of the architect's voice, only for them to fly open at his much louder, "What?" because I know that voice. And he isn't happy in the slightest at whatever she's just told him, which I'm sure was about who's here looking at this house.

At the sound of heavy footsteps heading this way, I scramble up out of the chair, on my feet a mere moment before Zach storms into the room and glares at me from where he stands in the doorway.

"You're not buying this house," he declares as the realtor walks up beside him, confusion all over his face as he points at me and turns his face to hers. "No sale."

"No need to be a dick, Zach." I cross my arms over my chest as she gasps and he returns to scowling in my direction, his eyes hard and matching the bitter twist of his lips. "I didn't know you were an architect, let alone that you designed this house."

"Bullshit." He takes a step forward and then glances back at the realtor. "I'd like to talk to...*her* for a minute, alone."

"Uh, sure. I'll see if your husband is done," she says to me, her eyes rounded as she rushes off toward the kitchen, visibly upset at the animosity between Zach and me.

He lashes into me the moment she's gone. Although he doesn't step any closer, each word is a slap of its own. "What fucking game are you playing, Darcy? Forget you exist? Pretend we never met? How the fuck am I supposed to do that when you're standing in *my* house?"

As much as I hate it, my voice comes out hushed as tears cloud my vision, even as I want to shout that it won't be his house much longer if he's selling it. "I didn't know it had anything to do with you, I swear. Oliver saw the listing yesterday and brought me here as a surprise."

Both his brows rise as he finally takes a step closer. "You searched for me, found my address, and didn't notice I'm the most sought-after architect in the entire fucking state?"

"No." I talk louder, finding my own anger inside me and letting it free once more. "No, I didn't. I was too pissed at your treatment to give a fuck about anything more than coming to your house and doing something about it instead of caring about what you do for a living."

His hands fall to his sides, some of the ire on his face replaced with remorse as he sighs and says, "I'm sorry. After what you said, I thought you were fucking with me by coming here."

"How insulting. I'm not a goddamned child nor am I that petty and I never have been."

Nothing except guilt on his face now. "I know. I—"

"Do you?" Interrupting, I take a step to the side and then hold up my hand when he attempts to get closer, making sure he sees the rings glinting in the sun because I don't like the sudden look in his eyes. "I'm *married*, Zach. My husband is in the kitchen. We're going to have a baby. I don't have the inclination, let alone the time to spite you—"

"What?" His face goes ashen, a reaction I don't understand at all because it's truly the one thing that has nothing to do with him. "You're pregnant?"

"Yes." I shake my head when he opens his mouth. "No, whatever you're going to say, don't. As soon as Oliver gets back, I'll tell him I don't want this house, and we'll find another. Just...leave before he comes back, please."

He strides forward at that, stopping in front of me before I can react to his approach, and lifts a hand to cradle my cheek as he smiles. The next words he speaks are soft and filled with an affection I haven't heard from his mouth since we were teenagers. "Congratulations, Darcy. I wish you two all the best, and you can have the house if you want it."

Such a sudden change from the way he's been behaving, making me wonder what the hell is happening and I want to ask him to tell me. I also should apologize, but the chance for either of those things to happen is prevented.

At the sound of the realtor's heels clicking against the floor as she returns, we spring away from one another even though we weren't doing anything wrong. Zach turns away and takes a few steps, but I make a misstep in my own heels when I go to sit back down, catching the corner of the carpet with my foot and barely managing to gasp before the wooden floor is rushing up at me.

The sound of Oliver shouting my name reaches my ears at the same time my head meets the corner of the coffee table on the way down, and everything goes dark before I've even hit the ground.

FOR A LITTLE WHILE, I HEAR PEOPLE TALKING around me, yet I can't make out anything in particular.

Then, suddenly, everything around me is silent, and the pain in my head is intense. I lift a hand to rub where I remember the table hitting me, only to find nothing wrong with it. Not even a bump.

Stranger than that, I'm not lying on the hard carpet covered floor, but a soft bed. Thinking I must've been out longer than a few minutes, I'm just about to open my eyes when someone touches me.

The hand — which seems pretty small so can't be Zach or Oliver's — pushes on my shoulder once, then again before a boy's voice mumbles something I'm certain definitely shouldn't be directed at me. "Wake up, Mom."

Gasping, I force my eyes open and sit up straight, whipping my head to the left to see who the hell thinks I'm their mother...and stare right into the vivid blue eyes of a boy with blond hair who can't be more than ten years old.

A kid who looks a little like me and a lot like Zach and who appears around the age our child would've been.

This can't be real.

I pinch myself, hoping this a dream, and I'll wake up from how hard I do it, but no. I feel the pinch with every part of me, and suddenly, it's clear something has gone suddenly, terribly wrong.

And instead of screaming or breaking into sobs — don't want to freak him out even if I want to myself — I swallow hard, smile at the kid and ask, "Where's your dad?"

"Making breakfast."

He says this as if I should know the answer and without waiting for me to respond, he leaves the room.

Climbing out of bed, I look down and discover I'm wearing the ugliest pair of fuzzy pajama's sporting rabbits I've ever seen. Walking over to the full-length mirror by the dresser, a sigh of relief rushes out at seeing my appearance is the same, although the circles under my eyes might indicate I either didn't sleep well last night, or it's a chronic problem.

Something tells me it's the latter.

Opening the drawers, I try to find something I don't hate to wear, and eventually pull out a tank, bra, and a nice pair of skinny jeans. Only the sight of my slightly curved belly when I take off my shirt means the jeans I took out seconds ago won't fit... and that I'm at least four months pregnant instead of just one.

None of this makes sense, and it's getting more disturbing by the second.

I put on the bra and tank, rummage through the drawer until a loose pair of yoga pants fit my requirements, and pull them on before heading out my door to find out what the fuck is going on, as I've apparently lost my mind.

My answer doesn't show up even when I arrive in the kitchen. No, it gets worse when I see the little boy standing by the stove next to *Oliver* and Zach isn't anywhere in sight.

Yet nothing prepares me for seeing my mother sitting at the center island as if she belongs there, talking to what appears to be a little girl who can't be more than three years old and has hair as red as mine.

Many things come to mind for me to say, and to ask, but the only thing I can manage is an angry question through my clenched teeth, "What the fuck are you doing here, Mother?"

Her head jerks up at the same time Oliver turns around, his own expression filled with shock, but I hear nothing when his mouth moves as sudden wooziness causes me to wobble where I stand and for what feels like the second time in minutes, I pass out on my way to the floor.

PART II

WHAT MIGHT'VE BEEN

"Is she drunk?"

The sound of my mother's voice asking that as I come to ruins any chance of her being a figment of my imagination and I decide to wait a little longer to let them know I'm awake, hoping this will all fade away.

But no, Oliver answers her with a light chuckle.

"She doesn't drink while pregnant," he says as the warm brush of his hand across my forehead brings me comfort, something I'm glad for in this confusing as hell situation. "Perhaps she was sleepwalking."

"Let's hope so," my mother retorts in her all too familiar disapproving tone. "That sort of language in front of the children is unacceptable."

Whether it's because he's touching me or because I know him so well, I *feel* Oliver's sigh to my bones as he replies softly, "She's been a little on edge lately...with the pregnancy and...well, you know."

"Both of your faults." My mother clucks her tongue, her displeasure with whatever she's referring to crystal clear. "I'm afraid I will never understand my daughter. I gave up many years ago and simply put up with her irrational decisions for the sake of my grandchildren."

Wow. As always, I can rely on my mother to point out how much of a disappointment her only child is to her.

"And you...I expected better from you," she continues on, scolding him. "However, as long as my grandchildren are loved and taken care of, that's matters more than anything else."

"Of course."

When Oliver doesn't say anything else — such as something that might give me insight into whatever the hell they're discussing — I decide now is the perfect time to "wake up" and determine what is going on. Turning my head toward the right — the side Oliver is on — I open my eyes and find him smiling down at me, eyes filled with worry.

His appearance is the same, yet there's something about him that's different from the man I've spent years with. Doesn't take me long to pinpoint the difference; his touch is firm, and there's a noticeable confidence in his gaze as well as his manner.

Squeezing my hand, he places the palm of his other one against my forehead as if to check my temperature. "You scared us. Are you feeling all right?"

"I'm fine." Noticing the pain in my head from earlier is gone, I return his smile, although mine is more unsure, and move my gaze to the woman I haven't seen in ten years standing not far from where I am. "Mother. You're still here."

"You must've hit your head harder than we thought," she comments, her lips pinching as she studies me for a few torturous and silent seconds. "Either way, I am not amused. You know damn well I live here and have since your father died a year ago."

No emotional reaction from me at her statement. No happiness or sadness that my father is no longer alive and now my mother lives with me because of it.

Bitterness rises in my throat and makes it way out as a scathing retort toward this woman who has never loved me like she should. "What? Is all your money gone? Because that's the only reason I can think of that you would choose to live with your disappointing and irrational daughter."

Her swift intake of breath and rounded green

eyes so like my own means she understands I heard what she said about me while not knowing I could hear them.

Before she can respond, Oliver shocks me into silence by grabbing my chin and bringing my gaze back to his as he hisses, "Stop, now. This isn't funny."

"I'm not laughing." Jerking my chin out of his grasp, I sit up and finally notice he must've carried me back to the bed before looking at my mother to say, "Get out."

She glares at me before huffing, "Fine. I'll go check on the children and make sure they aren't traumatized from your bizarre behavior earlier."

"Bitch," I mutter as she leaves the room, shutting the door behind her with a decided snap.

"What is your problem today?" Oliver releases my hand and stands up, his whole expression one of disgust as he frowns at me. "Your cruelty toward your mother is inexcusable after everything she's been through."

"Excuse me?" Tossing aside the blankets, I get out of bed on the other side and mirror his stance, not sure who is the angrier one between us. "What exactly has she been through?"

Instantly, his face falls into concern, all traces of anger gone. "Are you ill? Did you hit your head harder than I thought and need to see a doctor?"

"No, my head is fine." Even though I'm sure this has to be a dream even with the pinch test, the last thing I want to do is end up with him or anyone else thinking me crazy by acknowledging there are things I don't remember that I obviously should. "Well, perhaps it's a little fuzzy from the fall, so just tell me what you're talking about."

He frowns but indulges me anyway. "You know your mother has no money. She spent everything she had on your father's experimental treatments, and they were broke by the time he passed away."

"Treatments?" The moment I ask the question, the information is suddenly there in my head, which is weird as fuck. I hold up a hand and stop him when he starts to respond. "Forget it. I just blanked there for a second."

Some facts about this...life, I guess...run through my head at full speed.

Apparently, my father had early onset Alzheimer's, diagnosed as Stage Two when he was sixty, and then he ended up dying of a heart attack. He was only sixty-five.

And my parents, who never cut me off as they threatened, have been in my life this entire time. That's why my mother moved in with me — no rift between us ever existed — and why my sudden hostility is shocking to her and Oliver.

Now I'm going to have to apologize even if I

don't understand a damn thing that's going on or why the hell I can't wake up from what has to be a dream. One that is so unbelievably real.

"You should eat something," Oliver says gently, coming around the bed to slip his hand into mine and my stomach grumbles at his words. "See? Come on, you'll feel better when there's food in you."

I let him lead me out of the room without another word, but mostly because with all the information in my head now, there's nothing about how I'm with Oliver and not Zach. Actually, there's no details about either of them at all, which is disturbing all on its own.

A quick rub of my ring finger on my left hand with my thumb finds two rings there, so we must be married. But that kid can't be ours even if he refers to Oliver as Dad; he looks too much like Zach for that to be possible.

Which leaves me with plenty of questions such as where is he? And what the hell happened between us?

I want to ask Oliver but don't because that's absolutely something I should know. Hopefully, it will come to me before Oliver decides I should see a doctor for my head.

Neither the kids nor my mother is in the kitchen when we enter. Oliver guides me to the table and returns with a plate of pancakes less than a minute later.

"Kept them warm for you," he says, grabbing the syrup and pouring me a glass of orange juice, before sitting down across from me and handing me a fork. "There."

I have a niggling sensation he does this often because he does it all so smoothly. Nodding, I start eating while he pulls out his cellphone, leans back in his chair, and taps at the screen while casting occasional glances in my direction.

Once I've taken the last bite and set down my fork, he puts the phone down on the table, reaches across the table, and covers my hand with his. "Are you okay for me to go to work or do you need me here for the pick-up in a bit?"

Not knowing what he's talking about, I simply ask in true confusion, "Why would I need you here for that?"

"Things between you and Zach have been hostile lately, and after the episode with your mother earlier, perhaps it's best I'm here when he picks up the kids for the weekend."

Oh, I see. Zach has visitation.

My heart races at that. It doesn't even matter why things are hostile between Zach and me; it won't be any different than how he acted before this whole bizarre dream, after all. What matters is that I will get to see him and perhaps figure out why we're not together.

I shake my head and smile at him. "No, you were right. I feel much better now that I've eaten. Go on to work."

"All right. You'll call me if you don't feel well again, though."

A demand formed as a request. I can't help but wonder what made this Oliver more confident than the one I know. Either way, I grab my plate and rise from my seat while nodding at him again. "Yes, I will. I promise."

"Good." He stands up, too, and comes close enough to pull me in for a soft, sweet kiss on the lips. "I'll be home by six."

I resist the urge to suck in a breath at the sudden butterflies in my stomach from his kiss. "Okay."

With that, he's gone, so I take my plate to the sink and then decide to wash all the dishes. It doesn't take long and when I'm done, searching for my cell phone is next as I'm sure it's here somewhere and will fill in some holes.

Finding it in the bedroom by the bed, I slide my fingers across the screen and am grateful it opens up without asking for a pin. I've yet to use one on a phone of mine but at this point everything is unsure.

Amazing.

My whole life is now at my fingertips — from over 1,000 photos to my email, as well as both a Facebook and an Instagram profile — and I go with the one most likely to tell me the vital stuff.

Sitting on the bed, I open up the app and click around until I'm on the about page of my profile. Married to Oliver Thompson since July 31st, 2014 shows up under my relationships and nothing else. Switching to Life Events, I glance over the details until I find what I want to know: Gabriel Benjamin Haider, born July 1st, 2007 and Abigail Roselyn Haider, born September 20th, 2013.

What?

I blink at the dates and wonder how the hell our daughter is Zach's, yet I married Oliver when she was just over ten months old.

Then, my stomach rolls and tightens as Oliver's words about how things have been 'hostile lately' between Zach and I take on a whole new potential meaning. Yet, another look at the date on my phone — August 26th, 2016 — shows we've been married over two years now, so why would things be hostile *recently* if it has been that long?

Nothing comes to my mind, however. No matter how much I stare at the information, the whole situation is a blank except for the tiny bit of knowledge I've found on my own.

Switching over to the photos on Facebook, the result is the same. Not a damn thing. Going back past two years, there isn't one single picture of Zach and me, just of the kids, me, my parents, and sometimes Oliver.

Of course, the more I search for something, anything, and don't find it, the more dread settles in the pit of my stomach and won't go away.

Why is the father of my children nowhere to be found in pictures dating back to their birth?

And why, as the doorbell chimes to probably announce his arrival, do I have the awful feeling whatever happened between us is more my fault than his in this life, too?

For the first time since kicking me out of the house I designed — and the one I happily let her keep in the divorce — Darcy opens the door when I arrive to pick up the kids for the weekend, and she doesn't glare at me.

Instead, she throws me off by greeting me with a smile. "Zach."

Stunned at the genuine pleasure on her face, I step inside when she moves back to let me in, and return her welcome once she shuts the door. "Darcy. Are the kids ready?"

Glancing toward the stairs, she clears her throat and then shrugs with a hesitant expression. "My mother is with them."

"Ah." Slipping my keys into my pockets, I cross my arms over my chest, intrigued with the sudden difference in Darcy's attitude toward me. "How's she doing?"

"Fine, I guess."

"Good."

As she stands there staring at me, her hands twisting together, it becomes harder by the second to ignore her unusual behavior.

Although I never took much notice of what she wore when we were married, it has been a good while since I've seen her in what anyone would call normal clothing. Usually, she wears her pajamas when answering the door, so until this moment her pregnancy hadn't been visible as it is now.

The fact the baby isn't mine is the worst part.

Because I shouldn't dwell on it, and she's suddenly being so nice, I say something certain to annoy her. I hope it will bring back the typical Darcy I'm used to as well as help me avoid saying something stupid. "Pregnancy looks good on you, as always."

"Thanks," she says, lifting her hands to place them on her stomach as her face colors at the compliment.

She's blushing? I haven't seen her do that since high school. What the fuck?

"Ah..." Since the kids aren't coming down, and she continues to stand there looking at me instead of going to get them, I nod my head toward the steps. "Mind if I go see if they're ready to go?"

"No, not at all. Go ahead."

"Thanks." In case she changes her mind, as she has plenty of times for many things, I leave her standing by the door and am upstairs in less than thirty seconds flat.

Her mother greets me when I'm halfway down the hallway as she walks out of Gabe's room.

"Zachary."

I always enjoy the way she says my name; she's never been able to completely remove all the disdain she feels from the word. "Paula."

This is the first time she's had a private moment with me since she moved in. She doesn't even take a breath before launching into a speech, which is one I'm sure she's been itching to share since her arrival last year.

"Ten years ago, I thought you were the worst thing to ever happen to my daughter. I was sure you killed any chance of her finishing her education and that she would never have a life similar to what she was accustomed. You proved both me and her father wrong by providing a wonderful life for her and the children; for that, I'm grateful." She purses her lips when I acknowledge her praise with a nod. "And then, when I heard you were getting divorced, there was no doubt in my mind Darcy must've done something to make it happen because you've never struck me as the sort of man who would want his family split up. But I was wrong."

"Things happen." And they do. Plus, I know she doesn't have the whole story because Darcy would never admit everything to her parents. "It's better this way."

"Is it?" She shakes her head, the disappointment she often leveled at Darcy now directed at me. "Why did you do it?"

Such a loaded question, but there's only one answer that matters. "Because her sadness made both of us unhappy."

"Oh, pish. Nobody's happy in their marriage all the time."

"That may be true for someone. However, she was miserable, and I knew the way she thought. She wouldn't leave because of the idea that a mother suffers for her children's sake, even if it isn't what's best for her."

"So, instead of counseling or spending more time together, you give her a *real* reason to divorce you and never look back. How mature."

She's wrong about both of those things. We spent plenty of time together, and when that didn't work, we went to quite a few counseling sessions.

But that's the one thing about feelings. Mine were stronger than ever; Darcy's weren't. And you can't breathe life into something that's been dead for longer than your spouse wants to admit out loud.

Have I kicked myself plenty of times for deliberately hurting the only woman I've ever loved just so she would be brave enough to leave a marriage she wasn't fulfilled in any longer? Yes, absolutely. It's been killing me every day since, especially as my actions broke her trust in me, but I freed her with the one thing I despise more than anything in the world — a lie.

One she'll never know the truth about and neither will her mother; not even if Darcy smiles at me like my arrival here is the happiest moment of her day as she did downstairs moments ago.

"She wanted him," I state flatly. "And we were done."

"If that's true, then why is she so angry over your upcoming wedding?"

I wish I knew, but it doesn't matter, and I give her mother the only answer I can think of. "Perhaps it's hard for her to imagine someone else becoming a mother figure to our children, the same way it was hard for me to acknowledge Oliver taking on that of a parental role when they are here at home."

With that, I hope the conversation is at an end, and it is as Gabe exits his room and steps into the hallway with his backpack filled to bursting on his back, ready to go as much as I am.

And Abby, her mother's daughter down to her attitude, appears a second later, flying down the hall in our direction while squealing, "Daddy!"

I crouch down, catching her tiny body in my arms to give her a hug, and then stand up again. "Say bye to your Grandmother."

They do, in a flurry of hugs and kisses, and we head downstairs to the car. As I open the door, they both run off to find Darcy to say goodbye to her, and she shocks me by returning with them to the foyer.

"I'll have them back on Sunday by six, as usual."

"Oh. Don't stress about it," she says with a wave of her hand. "I'm hardly going to be mad about you being late when you're spending time with them."

Huh. Unbelievable.

I don't know what to say because getting mad when I keep them over the time is exactly what she does, citing how it puts them behind schedule for bed that night, which also messes up things for her.

Considering they will be returned on time, I don't say anything at all in response to her complete one-eighty and nod as the kids walk past me out the door. "All right. See you then."

"Yeah." She puts her hand on her stomach and gazes at me with the same soft look from earlier. "See you."

I head out, shutting the door behind me with a soft click, and after a bit of rationalization on my part, I chalk up her softened attitude as a result of her finally coming to terms with my re-marriage and put all my focus on where it should be for the rest of the weekend — enjoying the time with my kids.

"I'm going out," my mother announces from the doorway of the kitchen shortly before dinner after not talking to me all day. "I hope you haven't forgotten and made more food than necessary."

Giving the pasta sauce another stir, I put down the wooden spoon and turn to her with a shrug. "Didn't make enough for you, but even if I did, what would it matter? That's what leftovers are for."

She raises both brows and crosses her arms over her chest. "Leftovers? Are you joking?"

No, of course not, but then again, I'm not in my normal life where I spent years making food last longer than one meal, and I guess wasting food in this one is no big deal. "Maybe I am."

"I hope so." She glances at her watch and then

grasps her clutch tighter. "I need to get going. Are you going to be all right until Oliver arrives home?"

"I'm not a child who needs someone to watch her all the time, Mother, but thank you for your concern."

I figure she will leave at that, but instead, she walks closer, her question filled with what I might call worry if I weren't used to a former version of her as she stops just short of where I'm standing by the stove. "Darcy, I don't know where this sudden hostility toward me is coming from. I know we haven't always gotten along, but I am still your mother, and I love you even if I don't understand you."

Yep, definitely not the same mother I've hated all these years. I may not know what the hell's going on or why I can't wake up back to my real life, but I'm going to have to work on being kind to her and everyone else until it happens.

"I'm sorry." Turning back to the stove, I pick up the spoon and stir the sauce again, glancing over my shoulder to see her smiling at me softly. "I guess I'm just having a bad day."

She doesn't seem bothered when I don't return her words of affection, squeezing me on the shoulder before saying. "It's all right. Tomorrow will be a better day. And I've got to go now."

I don't think it is all right, but as with many

others things since waking up here, I don't say that. "Okay. Enjoy your evening."

No further response from her as her heels click across the floor, and less than ten seconds later, the back door opens and shuts as she leaves for wherever she's going.

That's when the freakout I've been holding in since waking up rushes out of me in the form of hiccuping sobs. I manage to turn off the sauce and the noodles, remove them from the heat, and then stumble toward the front of the house.

After Zach stood in the foyer staring at me as if I've grown two heads, I spent the whole day searching as quietly as possible for information on what happened between us but haven't come across anything so far. Not even divorce papers, which have to be around the house somewhere.

Then, after climbing the steps, I realize there is one place I haven't looked: the attic. I figured out where the door was earlier but hadn't gone up there because of my mother's presence, and not wanting her to ask me what the hell I was searching for.

After the tears subside and my face is dry, I open the door, flip the light switch, and take the narrow steps, crouching down upon reaching the top because the attic is more of a crawl space thanks to the low beams.

And there sit a few boxes not far from where

I've entered the area; only one of them has my name on the side of it. Sitting down, I yank the box in my direction, open the flaps, and discover that everything Zach had been shoved into this box before being put out of sight.

Pictures galore fill the box. All the ones missing from the past on Facebook are all here in this box, printed and kept in quite a few photo boxes. Then, the mementos, from dates and anniversaries I don't remember.

And finally, a folder filled with a stack of papers, with the final judgment for divorce on top, telling me all about our marriage. A marriage that began nine days after our son's second birthday and officially ended on December 20th, 2013, when our daughter was only three months old, with 'irreconcilable differences' cited as the reason.

Never hated a term more than I do right now as those two words that can mean anything stare at me all while my brain refuses to conjure up what those differences were. After just shy of three and a half years of marriage and eleven years together total, what the hell happened?

And I hate the blanks. Is there a point to getting some information and not what I consider the real important stuff, such as knowing what the hell happened between me and the man I defied my parents for?

Why aren't the empty spaces filling in like earlier?

"Darcy?"

Jumping at Oliver calling out to me from downstairs, I shove everything back in the box and close the flaps, pushing it back to where it was before heading back down the steps.

Finding him in the kitchen, he turns toward the door when I enter and points at the now cold food in the pans on the stove with a chuckle. "Guess this isn't what you wanted for dinner?"

Then, his whole expression changes to one of worry as he looks me in the face. Walking over to me, he cups my cheek as he stops in front of me. "What's wrong?"

"Nothing is wrong."

"Your eyes are puffy and red from crying and you don't cry for no reason."

"Maybe I did today."

I need him to believe that because I can't possibly tell him the truth; he would think me insane and if he didn't, I would wonder about his sanity.

Wrapping his arm around my waist while the hand on my face slips around to the nape of my neck, he shakes his head and sighs. "All right, I'll believe you for now, because I'm starving and have decided to take you out for dinner."

I hear him yet all response stops short of exiting my mouth, every inch focused on his hold and the way my heart beats faster with each second. Awareness of the attraction between us quickly evolves into desire sparked, arousal and need for Oliver that I've never experienced before flooding all of my senses.

Swaying toward him, my hands fist his shirt, anchoring me at the same time he tugs me closer until our clothed bodies touch everywhere possible. His mouth is dangerously close to mine now, making my own lips tingle with anticipation as his gaze drops to them, and all thoughts of dinner disappear as he leans in to give me what my eyes and body are begging for.

A light brush, the first stroke of a slow and steady seduction intended to drive us both mad. My mouth gives way to the pressure of his with a gasp, his tongue making love to mine in a dance my body remembers even if I don't, and I curse the clothes preventing us from getting any closer to one another.

He must have the same idea because he rips his mouth away, lifts me in his arms and waits until I wrap my legs around his waist before practically growling, "Fuck dinner."

Carrying me out of the room and up the steps, he resumes ravaging my mouth as if we've done this a million times and leaves me with no doubt about why we ended up married and now have a baby on the way.

The 'how' of it continues to elude me, but it becomes the last thing I want to think of as Oliver strips my clothing off and unknowingly demonstrates what a little confidence on his part would bring to our bed in my real life.

WE FINALLY GO OUT FOR DINNER NEARLY TWO hours later to an amazing local restaurant where tables line the perimeter of the room and couples can dance in the center.

Oliver stands up after the waiter takes our drink order, holding out a hand and saying with a twinkle in his eyes, "Dance with me."

I shake my head. "I'm no good at dancing."

"Funny." He grabs my hand and tugs me up from my seat, leading the way onto the floor before turning to me with a smile. "Let's see if we can remember how to do this, hm?"

He pulls me closer, sliding his right hand to rest on my lower back while leaving a bit of space between us. Instinctively, I put my left hand on his shoulder, and our free hands meet in the air, our fingers interlacing.

Amazing. I've never known how to dance and have taken no lessons, yet here I am, dancing while following his lead. Our bodies are in sync, our movements graceful, and the fact we're dancing without stepping on each other's toes makes me laugh out loud.

Oliver grins at me and pulls me even closer until our bodies are almost touching, leaning in to press a soft kiss against my mouth before quietly commenting, "All those classes and we haven't danced since our wedding. We need more evenings like this."

Ah, dance classes. That explains it.

Not knowing what to say to that since I hope I'll wake up tomorrow and not be here, but because this is enjoyable, I simply say, "Yeah, this is nice."

And the dance is over too soon as we return to our table when the song ends. The waiter arrives with our drinks and takes our dinner order, after which Oliver takes a few sips of his before reaching across the table to hold my hand.

He's sweet like that throughout dinner and on the way home, always making sure I'm comfortable. His excitement for the baby is endearing and identical to his attitude in my real life...enough I start to feel guilty for not actually being the woman he married.

And for the first, as we head home, it dawns on me.

What's happening in my real life if this isn't a dream? Is the me from here in that life? Or am I in a coma?

By the time we're inside the house, this whole situation is finally driving me insane, to the point I want to tell him I'm not his wife and explain what the hell is going on.

His reaction isn't what I'm afraid of, not really.

No, the truth is, I fear being stuck here in this life I don't understand and didn't participate in, and what might happen if I say something.

So I remain silent as we both get into more comfortable clothing before relaxing on the couch in the living room to watch a movie.

He invites me to snuggle against him, and I do.

It isn't long before I lie down with my head in his lap and promptly drift off as his hand rests on my shoulder with its warm and familiar weight.

Here, with him, is the freedom to let down my guard, even if only to get some much-needed rest.

THE NEXT MORNING, I WAKE UP SNUGGLED UP to Oliver in bed, with no recollection of how we ended up there, and am instantly sad at not having returned to my life.

He rouses when I attempt to get out of bed without waking him, but other than a quick moan of protest, he releases me before sitting up as I rest on the edge of the bed.

"Morning, sleepyhead," he says in a drowsy voice filled with affection. "Give me twenty minutes and I'll make breakfast."

"I can do it." Standing, I lift a robe off the chair and find him watching me, his expression bemused and pleased all-in-one. "What?"

"You haven't made breakfast in a long time. But," he puts up a hand while rising and then stretches both arms above his head. "I won't stop you because I've always loved your cooking."

Haven't cooked? I don't ask. "Okay."

He comes around the bed, pecks his lips against mine, and then walks over to the dresser. "I'm going to get a shower. See you downstairs." Then he stops, turns to grin at me, and asks, "Unless you want to join me?"

My body says yes, but my head says no, and I shake it. "Ah, go ahead. I'm really hungry so better get started."

"All right."

He walks off, not sounding disappointed at all,

and for a moment, I stare at him with wonder. Strange. Weird. And definitely a little crazy that his complete difference from the man I've been friends with for eight years bothers me and not in a good way.

I like familiar. Routine. Oliver's always needed me as much as I needed him. We are each other's stability, but this one?

He wants me. Doubt he needs me, at all. He's comfortable taking me as I am, and not even a little bizarre behavior on my part seems to bug him for long.

Honestly, he probably chalks it up to being pregnant, and it wouldn't surprise me if Zach and my mother had done the same yesterday.

I have to keep in mind that this version of Oliver is different, as is my mother. Can't be certain about Zach yet. He watched me yesterday, though, and I knew the things I said were surprising him — the slight flaring of his eyes and twisting of his mouth gave him away.

What I hate is not knowing why he was reacting that way; the mystery of our breakup is obviously relevant to his actions.

So much to discover about these two relationships and doesn't seem like it's going to just show up in my head. I may have to straight out ask or find someone who will talk about everything without me asking...which is, of course, quite unlikely.

Sighing, I head downstairs and into the kitchen, searching through the cupboards to see if there's any pancake mix.

There is, and before long, I've got a stack of them finished. Turning off the stove, I finish cleaning up the small mess I made and carry the plate over to the table, then get the syrup from the fridge along with two glasses from a nearby cupboard.

Oliver walks in as I'm setting them on the table, fresh from his shower with damp hair and wearing nothing more than a pair of basketball shorts, which allows me to appreciate his physique. He isn't too muscular and his abs don't show, but it's obvious he works out and takes care of himself by his flat stomach.

And the way he can lift or carry me without breaking a sweat speaks well to his stamina.

"Smells wonderful," he observes, winking as he notices me staring at him and taking a seat at the table as I pour orange juice into our cups.

"They do." Blushing at being caught, I turn to put the orange juice back in the fridge, returning to sit across from him and smile while putting two of the pancakes on my plate. "Yesterday I didn't really eat anything except breakfast and dinner, but this morning, I'm starving."

"Well, good, since you're eating for two." He takes a bit of his food and smiles at me after swallowing it. "You seem better than yesterday. Did you get more sleep?"

"Yeah, I think so." Noticing I don't recall seeing my mother's car last night when we returned home, I frown at him and ask, "Do you know where my mother went last night?"

He laughs and takes a drink of his juice. "More blanking today?" When I just stare at him, he clears his throat and looks downright amused. "You really don't like her new boyfriend, do you?"

Oh...and crap. Hard to pretend everything is normal when I don't fucking know anything. I force out a light-hearted laugh and shake my head. "Of course I do. I'm just teasing you."

He nods and goes back to eating, all while I eat with my eyes focused on my plate, trying to keep from saying something else I should obviously know.

But a boyfriend? My father's been dead a year, and she's already seeing someone else. Okay, he was sick for a while before he died, yet still, I can't imagine being ready to date only after someone I had been with for a while, someone I *loved*, had died.

Oliver finishes before me and goes to wash his plate before coming back to kiss me on the cheek. "I'm going to go find something to watch on TV. Join me when you're finished?"

"Okay."

It isn't until he leaves the room that I wonder what Zach is doing, and that's when I think about the kids...for the first since he left with them.

I'm not used to having kids but still feel like a shitty person for not even thinking about them, as well as feeling nothing when it comes to the two children I had with Zach.

Disgusted, I finish up eating and wash my plate before going to let Oliver know I'm going to call and say hi to the kids, understanding it won't be good for anything more than making me feel better about not really being the mom they know and love.

12

ZACHARY

When I return with the kids at six o'clock on-the-dot Sunday evening, Oliver answers the door and smiles as both the kids say, "Bye, Dad!" before running past him into the house without even glancing back at me.

I'll never get used to that. They have fun at my house, but they always miss Darcy and are raring to go when it is time to head home every weekend.

That and they don't like my fiancée, Jen. Mostly because they only recently met her, after I was certain about marrying her and proposed, so they aren't comfortable with her as they were with Oliver when he married Darcy. The man's been in our lives since they met during a semester abroad during their final year of college and became best friends.

A semester where I worked my ass off while my parents helped me with Gabriel so my wife didn't have to miss out on a great opportunity.

It's hard not to wonder what might've happened between Darcy and me if she hadn't gone and they had never met. Not that he went after her — no, it was all her. She didn't cheat, but her feelings slowly changed over the years, until one day she looked at him the way she always had at me.

We tried everything to get us back to where we were. However, in the end, there hadn't been anything to do except give her what she wanted even if she wouldn't admit it out loud.

"Hey, man," Oliver says, returning his gaze to mine after watching the kids run down the hall and interrupting my thoughts. "Did you need to speak with Darcy? She's on the computer."

Back to avoiding me, then. All right, I can deal with that.

Shaking my head, I tell him, "No, need to go as Jen is waiting on me. Tell Darcy I'll see her on Friday, as always."

"Of course. Have a nice night."

"You, too."

He shuts the door with a final nod, leaving me standing outside the house that's mine no longer as he heads back to the life he's built with the woman I wish I could stop loving.

"WHAT DO YOU SUPPOSE SOMEONE WOULD CALL a woodchuck if it couldn't chuck wood anymore?"

My lips twitch at Jen's question as I slip out of my coat after arriving at her place and hang it in the closet by the door. "I suppose just chuck," I reply with a kiss to her lips, wrapping my arms around her waist as she slips hers around my neck. "Where do you get all these crazy questions from?"

"Just random thoughts," she says with a soft laugh. "Usually brought on by random memes I find on Facebook. You should try it sometime."

"Nah, I'm good without all that stuff."

She steps back and sticks out her tongue playfully. "You know, one day your kids will be on 'that stuff' a lot."

She uses her fingers to quote me before whirling away with a sigh when I merely shrug because social media just isn't my thing and never has been. Darcy was bugged by it, too, because I never wanted my pictures on the Internet either, not even when she assured me just her family and friends would see them.

I figured if they want to see us, they could come

to our house. Apparently, that was unreasonable. Not sure how considering our families had never been more than twenty minutes away by car, tops.

Trailing her into the living room, she sits down on the couch and pats the seat beside her, waiting until I'm comfortable before straddling my lap.

Her hands find the edge of my button-down and slip beneath it to touch her cool hands to the hot skin below. Smirking as I suck in a breath, she asks, "How was your weekend?"

With the exception of the time she spends with us, which has only been a few hours here and there for two months now, we don't talk to each other when I have the kids. It's alone time with the kids until we're married and something I'm glad she's never had a problem with.

"Good. The kids had a lot of energy as always. I don't remember having as much as they do when I was a kid."

"I bet you did." Her hands roam higher as mine rest on her bare thighs, just beneath the edge of her cotton shorts, and she giggles. "You can be pretty energetic yourself; I've had the aching body to prove it quite a few times."

"I do aim to please."

She smiles, getting as close as possible to rest her head on my shoulder, and nips at my neck. Then, she whispers in my ear, "How about you aim to please right now and slide those hands a little higher so the real fun can begin?"

God, I love this woman.

She's random and funny and is a teacher at the elementary school. She knows my children come first, and she's beyond patient when things don't go according to plan. She's independent, sexy, and isn't clingy.

I'm lucky to have met her and even luckier she wants to marry me.

Hell, I want to marry her.

Our wedding is in two weeks, and part of me is thrilled because I love everything about her.

Then, there's another part of me that, for just a moment, wonders whether I'm making a mistake I can't take back; that marrying Jen closes the door on Darcy and me forever.

But, the reality is, the door is already shut, sealed and cemented over.

I need to accept it. Have to.

Because the girl I fought for, had a family with, and built my life around is married to someone else and having his child. There is no us, not anymore, and never will be again.

My future is sitting on my lap and nuzzling my neck, waiting for me to respond to her question.

So, instead of brooding any longer, I make my future wife hold on tight as I stand up and carry her toward the bedroom to pleasure her until neither one of us can move.

MY PARENTS LEAVE THE ROOM TO TAKE THEIR seats in the chapel, giving me a few moments alone before taking my place at the end of the aisle.

Five minutes until our wedding begins and Jen becomes my wife. Hard to imagine, even two years ago, when I thought marriage would never be in my cards again.

Yet here it is, a second chance, and I'll do my damnedest to make it my last.

There's a knock at the door as I walk toward it to head to the chapel, and after straightening my tie, I swing the door open with a smile.

Only it disappears at the sight of Darcy standing there with reddened, watery eyes, her lips wobbling with the effort to suppress any further emotions from spilling forth.

The part of me that continues to love her wants to ask why she's upset. I don't, because she's not mine to comfort anymore, and the last thing I need to do right now is touch her when I'm about to marry someone else.

She merely stares at me as if she's unsure, in a

way she hasn't been since our teens, until I feel forced to ask, "What are you doing here, Darcy?"

"This is real," she whispers, walking past me into the room and over to the window, standing there without elaborating.

Against my better judgment, I shut the door, lean on it, and release a hard breath while crossing my arms over my chest. "Darcy? Answer me."

"This is real," she repeats while turning to face me and swiping at the tears sliding down her cheeks. "This life. This pregnancy." She inhales, deep and shuddering, as if her heart is breaking right this second, and lets it out slowly as her sorrowful eyes finally meet mine. "Us being no more because of me."

"What?" I shake my head and push off from the door, striding toward her. "It wasn't you, it was me."

Her eyes flash as I stop a few steps away from her. "Don't lie to me. You never condoned lying so don't you dare. Admit the truth, Zach, right now."

She knows? That isn't possible.

"Darcy, I don't know—"

Tears flow down her cheeks once more. "Stop it."

There isn't a chance in hell that I'll say what she wants to hear now.

She wanted out to the point she believed my lie, and now we'll both live with that forever. We both deserve to be with someone loves us as much as we love them.

I glance back at the door and then meet Darcy's gaze with a stern, "Jen's waiting on me, Darcy. I need to go."

She doesn't let me go, though.

Before I can move or push her away, she steps forward, throws her arms around my neck, and presses her soft mouth against mine.

13

DARCY

Two weeks of waking up in this life and wondering if it will ever end; needing it to end.

I've pieced together most of my life so far from searching through things, mostly on Facebook and in a few old notebooks, and don't really like what I've found.

I kept the pregnancy and Zach graduated. He worked full-time and went to school part-time while I finished high school after giving birth to Gabriel.

Zach ended up dropping out of college to work full-time in construction, while my parents paid for my school and I went full-time.

We got married just before I entered my senior year and apparently I studied abroad for a semester in Paris, which is where I met Oliver.

The idea we met abroad is weird to me. How had that happened? Oliver hadn't gone abroad in my real life where we met as freshman. And neither had I, obviously.

Since that moment, I've been bothered by the idea Oliver's life is radically different here because he met me later. And because we hadn't clung to each other to our detriment, he'd had to put himself out there, hence the improved confidence.

Either way, we stayed friends after the experience abroad and out of all the jobs he applied to before meeting me, he ended up taking the one with the best offer after graduation.

A job that put him within thirty minutes of where I lived with Zach and our son, in our hometown rather than across the country where I saw him in the bookstore that day.

There's nothing telling me how Oliver and I went from being friends to being married, though. I still have no idea, and now my ignorance of these facts is starting to bother me.

I'm going to ask Oliver after work tonight and hope he doesn't think I'm crazy. A part of me believes he won't — I can tell he isn't sure what to make of me. Every day, he's giving me funny looks and asking me if I'm all right when I say or do something that seems strange to him.

But even if he does think I'm insane, I can't keep on being clueless about this whole situation.

I've had plenty of free time, too. Apparently, I have a Bachelor's in Marketing and haven't worked since last year. Why? I don't know. Nothing indicates I was fired so my best guess is I left my job to be at home with Abigail and of course, now me and Oliver are having a baby of our own.

My mother hasn't been around much, and when she is, neither of us really seem to have much to say to each other. She eats with us when the kids are here and leaves for the whole weekend to stay with her boyfriend when they're not.

I've yet to meet him and can't decide if I even want to because while my father and I had our differences, I loved him. Seeing my mother with anyone else might hurt, a bizarre idea all on its own considering everything that's gone on between us.

As for Zach...he picked up the kids this morning while remaining short but polite with me and then left after saying he would see me on Sunday. He did the same last weekend — barely speaking to me and trying to leave with the kids as quick as he could, making me wonder what I did.

The way he acts has convinced me we're not together because of me, just like in my real life.

Can't get anything right, it seems.

Sighing, I head downstairs to change over the

laundry from the washer to the dryer, start another load, and hope Oliver comes home soon.

"Wow."

Oliver's face is a mix of astonishment and disbelief as he sits beside me on the couch later in the evening, trying to process everything I've just finished telling him.

The longer he stares at me saying nothing, the more I want to fill the silence, take it all back out of anxiety and fear he's thinking his wife has lost her mind.

"So," he finally says, drawing the word out while extracting one hand from where they hold mine to rub his chin and then he clears his throat. "You don't know anything at all?"

Blinking, mostly because I can't believe he's so calm, I bite my lip and shake my head. "No. Well, I've managed to put a few bits together, but anything about me and you..."

"Ah." He nods and lifts a knowing brow. "Just us, or Zach and the kids, too?"

"Only what I could gather from Facebook and the box in the attic."

"All right." Covering my hands again, he smiles and lifts them to his mouth, kissing the back of one of them before he says with a laugh, "Let me fill in the blanks for you, then."

My relief is palpable as I ask, "You don't think I'm crazy?"

"Surprisingly, no." He smiles when I lift a skeptical brow. "It explains a lot, especially the reaction at seeing your mother...and staring at me as if you don't know me at all most of the time. Am I really that different?"

Easy. Too easy. This must be a dream, but I'm gonna go with it. "Here, you are the man you could be there if you believed in yourself more. I'm not sure what to think about the role I've played in that."

He shakes his head and gives my hand a squeeze. "I don't think you should blame yourself for what others choose to do or how their lives ended differently. In my case, by the time I met you, you were already a mother. Confident, beautiful, and outgoing. You didn't need me or anyone else, which is one of the things I love most about you."

My heart beats faster at his words, tears springing to my eyes at the love shining in his eyes and words.

That sounds so lovely...for a moment, I wish *this* one as my real life and the other nothing more than a nightmare. Of course, it isn't, and I let the tears fall then because for the first time ever, I think the choice I made at sixteen wasn't the right one.

And Oliver, the husband who loves me no matter what form I'm in, wraps me in his warm and comforting embrace while I finally let myself feel the weight of the decisions I've made and the resulting consequences.

We stay that way for quite a while.

"You changed our relationship," Oliver informs me later in the evening after I've stopped crying and we've eaten dinner. "You were married to Zach when we met, a boundary I always respected."

Not off to a good start since this is inching toward everything being my fault. "But you had feelings for me?"

"Yes, something I never admitted, however, and we began spending less time together as things got busier in our lives."

"Okay. I wasn't happy about that, was I?"

"No." He laughs. "You were pissed. That's when I realized you perhaps felt more than friendship for me, too. So, I used work as an excuse to stay away even more, because I didn't want to be blamed for breaking up your marriage."

"I see. What happened?"

"The trouble started in January of 2013, shortly after you discovered you were pregnant with Abby. Zach began working more, having problems with all sorts of projects while expanding his business, and since you were working as well, he hired someone to assist with helping around the house. That seemed to ease things for a bit, at least when it came to household stuff, and you two spent more time together."

He shifts in his seat next to me on the couch, his hands in his lap as he sighs and continues when I nod.

"It was shortly after your Fourth of July party that you called me crying. You two got into an argument, and you asked me what to do. When I suggested you two should get marital counseling, you had the most bizarre reaction — cussed me out, told me there was no way you were going to do that, and hung up on me."

"What? That's crazy."

"Like I said, bizarre. From the moment we met, you were crazy about him. Proud of the way you stood up to your parents and had Gabriel against their wishes, and the fact you two made it more than a couple years when they thought you wouldn't." He shrugs. "I don't know what happened, but after a few weeks of not talking, you called me to say both of you were in counseling after all. When you said we shouldn't see each other for a while, it became clear you finally admitted your feelings for me, and I agreed staying apart would be best for us both."

His whole expression takes on a sadness as he looks up at me and reaches over to take my hand in his. "We didn't speak again until the day you went into labor with Abby. You were hysterical, saying you couldn't get ahold of Zach, and you didn't want to go to the hospital by yourself. So I came to get you, took you to the hospital, and when it came time to have her, he still hadn't arrived. You cried and begged me to stay in the room until I relented. He didn't arrive until hours after she was born and you blew up on him even after he explained there had been an emergency on one of his sites."

My heart hurts just listening to this. After seeing Zach with his kids, I can imagine how much missing his daughter's birth hurt him. He never would've done it deliberately. "Wow. A perfect storm, huh?"

"Yes. I've never seen you so angry in all the years I've known you. But that wasn't the final straw. That came a few weeks later when I visited you and the kids at your insistence. We were watching TV with Gabe while Abby slept in your arms when Zach walked in, took one look at both of us, and walked right back out."

He blows out a breath, making it clear the bad part is about to come, and says, "You handed me Abby, got up, and went after him. A good ten minutes later, you returned with tears streaming down your face and walked right past me into the kitchen without saying a word. Zach hadn't returned, so I put Abby in her swing, left Gabe watching the movie, and came to see why you were crying.

"When I entered, you were sobbing into your hands. Eventually, you looked up and simply said, 'He cheated on me.' That was it. He moved out the next day and when you filed for divorce, he gave you everything you wanted."

It wasn't the explanation I've been expecting. All the thoughts in my head rearrange with this new information as he stares at me, waiting for a reaction, and finally, I shake my head because this doesn't make sense. "That's not possible. Zach hates cheaters and liars."

"You never questioned it." He glances away as if considering why I hadn't before gazing back at me and releasing his hold on my hand. "Frankly, neither did I, but our feelings got in the way of any rational thought on the matter, in my opinion."

"Obviously, since it wasn't even seven months

between the divorce being final and us getting married."

"Your idea." He laughs at my gasp and leans in, kissing my mouth before smiling against them, then backs away again while my lips tingle. "You went back to being the woman everyone knew and loved after he left. No more sadness or anger, and a month after the divorce, you asked me on our first official date; said you weren't going to waste time. And I didn't say no because you were the woman I loved and desired. Still are."

I smile, then bite my lip and frown. "I don't understand. With everything you've told me, why are things suddenly so hostile between me and Zach, then?"

"You disapprove of Jen because he's only known her for a year and they're getting married on Sunday."

Something inside me shifts at this news, but there isn't any pain, just sadness. An 'oh' of acknowledgment and acceptance because of course he would move on and find someone else, just as I had.

And suddenly, I question everything — from this life and the real one.

Here, Zach's marrying someone else and I'm with Oliver, pregnant.

There, I'm with Oliver and pregnant too, while Zach's divorcing his wife.

Does that mean Oliver and I are supposed to be together, not me and Zach? At least, not for longer than the time we managed to spend with each other in both?

Or are our lives a reflection of choices we've made that we now can't take back without hurting others?

I don't know, but this whole situation is made worse by the fact that I'm not *this* Darcy, and the one I am has unresolved feelings for Zach.

But, what can I really do?

After all, he'll be somebody else's husband come Sunday.

"Are you all right?" Oliver's question cuts through my thoughts, and when I nod, he stands up and holds his hand out to me, completely oblivious to the uproar inside my head. "Let's go to bed. We'll talk more in the morning."

Deciding this is probably the best way to avoid me saying something inadvisable, I take his hand without another word and follow him toward the bedroom.

A bit later, even as Oliver falls asleep with me snuggled against him and his hand resting on my stomach where I carry our child, all I can think about is how Zach needs to tell me the truth.

And I'm going to make him because if I am stuck here in this life that isn't really mine, one where we're both living a lie based on the one he told, he's going to admit what he's done.

The possibility he actually cheated doesn't even enter my mind.

OLIVER HASN'T WAVERED AFTER MY confession. It's strange for him to believe me without hesitation, yet if I really think about us... well, maybe it isn't.

He's never been one to shy away from the strange and unexplainable, nor from flat out saying that telling Zach anything would be nothing short of disastrous, something I can't disagree with after having thought it over.

I still want to hear Zach admit he lied, though. For my own reasons more than anything else — he hated my lies, and now I understand the sentiment.

No matter what I wanted in this life, his lie prevented anything else from happening except what came out of his deception.

Just as I got an abortion in the absence of his consent, he ended our relationship here without mine.

But, when I woke up this morning, I decided to

let it go and arrive at his wedding with nothing more than to show support. Not for him, but for our children, who are going to have this woman in their lives as a stepmother.

Yet, the longer I sit next to Oliver among everyone else there for the wedding, waiting for Zach to take his place at the end of the aisle, the harder it is to breathe in the face of what's about to happen.

"I need to go to the bathroom."

I abruptly stand up and whisper this to Oliver, who thinks nothing of it and releases my hand with a smile and a muttered, "Hurry back. Supposed to begin in less than five minutes."

"I will."

But I don't.

Everything becomes a blur through the pain in my head and the tears streaming down my face. One moment we're talking, with him refusing to admit what we both know he's done, and the next, our lips are locked together.

And the lack of feeling stuns me.

No thrill, or passion, or heat between us. Not even when he groans and embraces me back, deepening the kiss as if he's trying to capture what we've always had and denying it doesn't exist with each sweep of his tongue inside my mouth.

Until the kiss is over as quickly as it began and he releases me at the same time I let go of his neck.

He makes sure I'm steady before stepping back, scrubs my taste off his lips with his hand, and glares at me as he growls, "Damn you."

I can't look at him even as I say the one thing I know to be true. "You lied to me." Even knowing and understanding why, the fact he would go so far as to hurt himself to make me happy kills me.

"I need to go," he says harshly, without acknowledging my accusation.

He doesn't have to, though, because that kiss said it all. His arousal had been hot and hard against my thigh as he ravaged my mouth, showcasing exactly how attractive he still found me all while his hold declared his love.

My body, the one that is mine yet isn't, feels nothing, but in my head, I'm the me who has never stopped loving Zach. And I want nothing more than to sob from the utter heartbreak swirling in his eyes when I finally meet his gaze again.

"I'm sorry," I manage to say while turning back to the window, unable to handle his pain or mine any longer, and say the word he's waiting to hear. "Go."

He does because there's nothing left to say.

I know the truth. We both do. And now we've freed each other.

The buzzing in my head grows to an unpalatable level then, both of my hands going to my head in an attempt to ease the accompanying throbbing.

It increases instead.

The last thing I remember as my vision darkens with the blackness rushing in is my hands flying away from my head to try and grip something while a scream is ripped from my throat.

Three days I've been waiting for her to wake up.

Even though I shouldn't, I've placed the blame for her fall in my hands.

And so had her husband the moment he found out who I was. He's questioned why I'm waiting around for her to wake up, telling me it would be better if I left and stayed away from Darcy now that they are married.

I can't fault him. He knows everything, of that I'm certain, and I would want me gone, too.

There's just one problem — the woman lying unconscious in a hospital bed is the one I've never forgiven or forgotten. I had a right to the way her decision made me feel, and I'll never believe she made the right one; but no, I honestly haven't ever looked past my own pain to understand hers...until recently.

Now, I have, making it imperative I apologize one more time — and this time I'll truly mean it.

After the other day, I know she needs it as much as I do, which is why I keep returning, hoping today is the day she'll open her eyes and allow me to wish her well.

Oliver walks out right as I'm about to leave for the night, needing to get back to Rose so Tara can go home, and stops me with an angry glare while crossing his arms over his chest. "She's awake and asked for you once she knew you were here. Don't upset her."

On the outside, I'm calm, giving him a cool nod before walking past him into the room. On the inside, nothing except turmoil from watching her fall and being unable to prevent it in time.

She's sitting up with her gaze locked on the door and smiles when she finally sees me. It's bright, her entire expression inviting despite how pale she is, and she holds out a hand as I reach the bedside.

"Hi," I say while clasping her hand in mine and taking a seat on the nearby chair. "I'm glad you're awake."

"Oliver said you won't stop coming back until you make sure I'm okay."

"You fell and hit your head in my house and have been passed out for nearly four days. Of course, I want to ensure you're all right."

"Afraid we're gonna sue you, huh?" She smirks at my instant frown because that thought hadn't even entered my mind. "I'm teasing. It wasn't your fault."

It's easier to breathe now with her appearing unharmed by what happened and I smile at her. "Glad your sense of humor remains intact."

"And my brain," she replies, laughing as she runs her hand through her hair and winces when she comes in contact with the bump on her forehead. "At least, I think so. Not sure after that wacky dream."

Her soft yet bemused expression prompts me to ask, "Dream?"

"Yeah..." Whatever she was going to say drifts away as she bites her lip and tugs her hand away. "It was something else, but I'm back now."

A rather bizarre thing to say that makes me more curious. "What did you dream of?"

She compresses her lips into a flat line, her eyes searching mine as if she's trying to decide what to do, and then shakes her head in conclusion. "It was nothing. Thanks for hanging around to make sure I was okay. With the way things have been between us..."

A perfect opening for what I want — no, *need* to say. "About that. I've spent the last ten years being angry at you and went so far as punishing you for it when I ran into you. And I know I've apologized for that already," I say, raising a hand to stop her from interrupting me, "but it wasn't good enough because I didn't believe the words when I said them the first time."

She tries to cut in anyway. "Zach—"

"No. Let me finish."

"Okay." She nods and places her hands in her lap after making a zipping motion with her fingers across her mouth.

It's hard for me to admit my weaknesses, but I plunge ahead because I don't have anything left to lose here. She's already out of my reach for good. "I'm not sorry for catching you following me that day. Or what happened after. I am, however, sorry for what I said and for placing all the blame on you, when we were both at fault for the whole situation. I went on and finished college, got a great job, and have a beautiful little girl who is my entire world. My marriage is a different story, but there's nothing I can honestly complain about, not after learning how hard things have been for you for way too long."

When a tear slips down her cheek, her hands

come up to her mouth, and she trembles visibly with the effort to keep from sobbing.

"I never wanted to make things worse for you or hurt you, regardless of what happened between us." Not resisting the urge to stand up, I lean over to take her into my arms as a tear slides down her cheek, but she stops me with a hand on my chest.

"Don't," she croaks out with tearful emotion as I sit once more. "Touching me in the first place is what got us into this mess."

Not expecting her to crack a joke, the abrupt laughter from myself catches me off guard, and so does her giggle as she wipes her face with both palms while taking a deep breath.

"Zach." She finally breaks the silence after calming down. "Apology accepted. After all, what else is there for either of us to do except put the past behind us and move on?"

"That's what I want, too. For us to forgive each other."

"Ah. Well, we don't need each other's forgiveness, Zach. Just our own." She gives me a sad smile and glances over my shoulder toward the doorway. "For ten years, I've punished myself, and I have to stop. I've got a husband and a baby on the way, and I can't build a life with all this guilt over something still weighing me down that can never be changed."

Hard for me to admit I wish our past could be changed. My feelings for her have been buried under a mountain of anger and with the way our attraction burns bright between us to this day, I know we would have had a great life together.

Tougher to let it all go, to free us both from the weight of our history, yet doing so is vital to both our futures.

A time in our lives that begins now and means this conversation has to end before I tell her what she's always meant to me...and always will, in complete honesty.

"You're right." Rising from the seat, I lean in, press a kiss to her cheek, and step away from the bed while glancing at my watch. "I need to get home to Rose."

Her eyes fly to mine then, her question wondrous. "Is that short for Roselyn?"

"You remember that?" At her sheepish expression, I laugh. "My grandmother would have loved her namesake."

She flicks her gaze away again, her voice softening. "She's adorable, Zach. I...I wish you both the best."

"And I want the same for you, Darcy. Take care of yourself."

"I will. Promise."

Her statement is filled with more conviction

than I've ever heard from her before and that's when I realize how civil this whole conversation has been.

I look at her; really examine her face for the first moment since walking in here and the transformation is amazing. Her expression is serene and more open. In fact, she reminds me of the Darcy I fell in love with rather than the unsure woman who followed me through a bookstore.

She does seem more peaceful already and seeing her this way hurts more than I'll ever admit to anyone.

With nothing more left to say that isn't superfluous or ill-advised, I put one foot in front of the other and leave the room, the profound sense of sadness settling in my chest.

Walking past Oliver, who gives me a brief and dismissive glance before heading back into the room, I make it all the way back to my car in the parking garage before recognizing what the ache truly means.

My love for Darcy never ended. I buried it under my hurt and pain and refused to think about her until she stopped entering my mind.

This revelation doesn't matter, though, because we are both different people from all those years ago, and I don't love her. I can't since I don't know her as she currently is, but I won't deny wishing I could find out, which won't and can't happen with the way things are presently.

Unlike when I ran into her at the store, I don't try to forget her or what we had. Instead, I get in my car and head home to my daughter, all while appreciating those few moments with Darcy for what they were: closure.

Then, I move on with my life, too.

Ever since Zach left without looking back, I've been determined to do the same.

Chalking up the whole other life experience as being nothing more than a dream has helped, because really, there's no way I would've been calm had it been real. And although I convinced myself that other Oliver's serene acceptance of my story had been in character for him, I doubt that's true, either.

So many misgivings about it that I actually haven't mentioned the dream to him at all, unlike the way I spoke about it to Zach without thinking about it. I was glad he let what I said go, though; not sure that would've gone over well with him either when all he wanted to do was make sure I was okay.

One thing I've learned is that decisions made

become permanent actions you can't undo, and each choice leads to the irrevocable consequences. There are ramifications for you and everyone you love even if you think the decision only affects you.

Something I wish I had learned long ago.

Everything seems so strange now. The dream appeared real and tangible, to the point I almost began to believe it was my real life. Weeks went by, but not even half a week had passed here. Crazy is how I felt for a few weeks after waking up, but that's slowly gone away.

Now, two months later, everything's back to normal, with the entire fall and hospital fiasco behind me.

I haven't seen or heard from Zach, and I can tell Oliver's quite happy about that. He hadn't been pleased with having him around at the hospital, nor had he liked finding out Zach built the house he was interested in buying. He swore if he had known, we wouldn't have gone to see it, but let the whole thing go when I reassured him it wasn't his fault or a problem, for that matter.

Despite Zach telling me we could buy it if I wanted, we passed on it and have continued looking for another. So far, nothing has caught both of our eyes, but that's okay because we have plenty of time until the baby arrives.

At fourteen weeks, I'm finally showing; the pregnancy easy and going well.

Oliver takes every chance he gets to rest his hands on or put his mouth close to my stomach. He talks, sings, and simply lights up with everything that involves our child.

He's going to make a magnificent father.

As for me, with my lack of experience with any children and the relationship with my own parents, I'm nervous about becoming a mother.

Actually, beyond anxious. More along the lines of terrified.

I've been thinking about it a lot and after that dream, or whatever it was, my parents have entered my mind more now than since the day I left home. Wondering how they are, if they're both alive and healthy, if they miss me, and if they would want to know their grandchild once I give birth.

The curiosity has been so intense that a few weeks back I dialed the home number to my parent's house — the one they've had since before I was born — and my mother picked up the phone. I didn't speak; I couldn't. I heard her voice and all the anger and hurt and yes, even the love I don't want to feel for her after everything...it was all there below the surface, just waiting for me to let it out.

She said hello twice before I lost my nerve and

hung up on her, tears streaming down my face for hours after as all the emotions I should've let out a long time ago came pouring out.

I meant, and still mean, what I said to Zach. I'm forcing myself to let go and move on. To heal, finally.

My child needs a mother who can deal with hurt, disappointment, and rejection, as well as a mother that has her shit together, at least more than I have in a long time.

Yes, I've come a long way from the girl who couldn't even fold her laundry or cook because her parents had servants who did all that, but I can admit that there are plenty of things left that need improvement.

As for Oliver? I want better for him, too. Everything affects both of us. His promotion helped a little, yet I've been working hard to make sure he gets out more so he can gain some confidence. It's amazing to see him make decisions without constantly asking me what I think we should do. Not that he doesn't ask for my opinion; just that now he trusts his own more than ever before and mine adds to it, rather than overrides his because of uncertainty.

That's why I love him more every day and am confident in my decision to marry him now. We're

growing together, and our life will be better than I could've ever imagined just a few months ago.

In some moments, it's easy to believe he and our unborn child will be all I need, but that's not true.

Reconnecting with my parents is necessary. Vital, really, if I want to shut down old hurts for good so I can truly move on and give them an opportunity to be involved in their grandchild's life.

It's just the question of when I'll get the nerve to let that happen now. Each day, tomorrow looks the better option, and I know the longer I take, the more chances tomorrow may be too late.

And through all that has happened, I don't want to chance being too late.

So, I pick up the phone and dial the one number there's no chance I'll ever forget.

When nobody answers, I hang up and barely suppress the urge to bawl my eyes out from the sudden disappointment I never expected to feel.

After no one had answered the phone, Oliver suggested we look for the information online. It was hard for me to say why I wanted to know if they were alive and living in the same place without telling him about the bizarre dream, but I managed.

Turns out my father is still alive and my parents live in the same house. This news has relieved a lot of my worry, yet a little bit of new anger has bloomed at seeing them all over their local news due to a charity they started three years ago — one that assists with pregnant teens who need somewhere to live.

The charity also provides support services so the mothers can keep their children.

Rationally, I know this is a great thing, as their guilt and regret at the way they treated me may have resulted in them helping others out. But, on the other hand, it hurts they haven't bothered to track down their own daughter and apologize.

Yet, once I found all this out, this last month has been spent wondering whether they didn't because of the way I told them to never talk to me again after they disinherited me.

So, here Oliver and I sit outside their house in a rental car a day before Thanksgiving while I try to convince myself to get out of the car and walk to the door.

"We can sit here forever, but they may wonder what the hell we're doing." He takes my hand in his and kisses the back with a smile as I laugh. "You're not going in there alone."

"I know. You just don't know my parents."

He clasps my hand tighter and smirks for an instant, then releases it to pull the key from the ignition. "I will when we get out of the car, walk to the door, knock on it, and then they answer."

"The maid will, actually."

"Darcy." His lips twitch as he grabs the door handle and makes the decision for me. "The longer we wait, the more nervous you'll be, so come on."

As he watches me, I take another deep breath and then after another minute in which I stare at the house with trepidation, finally nod while opening my door. "Okay, I'm ready."

We both get out, and he takes my hand as we walk up to the front steps, stopping in front of the wooden double doors with its fancy handles I remember. Oliver presses the doorbell with his left hand while gripping my hand in his with the other and tugs me closer to his side.

My mother's the one who opens the door in less than a minute, not the maid.

And Oliver attempts to ease things without missing a beat. "Mrs. Bechel, I hope it's all right we've just come here without calling first."

She inclines her head at his statement but doesn't even look at him, her eyes glued to mine.

The words I've thought about yelling at her the whole way here stick in my throat as she stares at me from the entryway, tears slowly starting to shimmer in her eyes.

She glances back and forth between Oliver and me, saying nothing as her hands slowly come up to rest on top of each other over her heart. Then, she finally speaks in a soft voice so unlike the one she spoke to me in for years. "I've been waiting for you to get out of the car since your arrival. I feared you would leave and never look back if I came outside to greet you."

I wanted to, even cried to Oliver as he pulled into the driveway that we should just act like we were on the wrong street and turn around.

As she takes a step closer to me in the tense silence hanging between us, I resist the urge to step back and finally manage to choke out, "You hurt me. The things you said and did after everything...I wasn't sure I could forgive you."

"I haven't forgiven myself, and neither has your father. We were wrong." She takes another step and moves her hands to rest on my shoulders, a tear sliding down both her cheeks as she whispers, "We were worried more about what our friends would think than we considered what was best for you, and for that, we're sorry. I know those words aren't adequate enough, but—"

"Mother." I shake my head to stop her while my own eyes water, tug my hand from Oliver's, and square my shoulders. "You're right. 'Sorry' isn't sufficient but thank you for the apology. We've all made mistakes and have learned from them. I think the best thing to do now is to move on, don't you?"

Her eyes round — probably shocked by how much I've grown up — as she swallows hard before saying, "Yes."

"Good, because we really want our son to have both sets of grandparents in his life."

What I've said takes a moment to settle in her head, but when it does, my mother embraces me with a gasp of delight as tears stream down both our faces now.

Oliver watches with a beaming smile on his face, his hand resting on the small of back in support.

When my father joins us on the porch not long after, he pulls both my mother and me into a hug with a sniffle of his own.

I cry even harder when he apologizes, too.

And even though I know we've got a long way to go to repair our fractured relationship considering it wasn't all that strong in the first place, for the first time since leaving home, I'm positive everything's going to be all right between us.

Five years later...

"Are you certain about this, darling? Your father and I will postpone the trip, if necessary." My mother blows her hair out of her face as she tapes up the last box of things and pushes it away from her. "If you're not ready, there's no shame in admitting it."

"I'll be fine."

Her expression is skeptical and filled with concern, for good reason.

Oliver's unexpected death the day before our son was born eight months ago hit all of us hard. He was only thirty-one, young and healthy. He didn't deserve to die and certainly not at the hand of a disgruntled and unstable ex-coworker who shot up the office in response to being let go for poor performance.

I could barely breathe the moment I found out, let alone function after, unable to cope in my shock and devastation.

My parents took care of everything and stayed on following the funeral to help out with the boys while I went to grief counseling. Their support from the moment we reconnected has meant everything to me.

And while nothing is as it was, nor will it ever be again, I've finally found a rhythm these past few months that I can live with.

So, after finding out my parents were going to pass on an eight-week European trip they planned a year ago because of me, I've made it clear they should go. Of course, they are worried no matter how much I try to reassure them, and since they leave tomorrow, this is my last chance to put my mother's mind at ease.

"I'll be fine," I say again with a smile this time. "I've got the boys to focus on and a job to search for. Oliver made sure we were taken care of, but it won't last forever."

She frowns. "You only do what you can handle and nothing more for now. And if you need anything, call us. We will return on the first flight available."

"For heaven's sake, Paula. Quit harassing the poor girl," my father tosses in with a laugh as he enters the dining room and puts his arm around my shoulder with a wink. "If she says she'll be fine, then leave her be and get ready so we're not running behind in the morning."

He definitely eavesdropped on the conversation before walking in. I put my arm around his waist and lean my head on his shoulder with a sigh. "Thanks, Dad. I want you two to enjoy your trip and not worry about me so much. You'll call every day anyway."

"Yes, we will, darling. Count on it," my mother tosses in while glaring at my father until he winks at her too and she gives in with a laugh. "All right, all right, Gil. I'm going to pack."

"Excellent," he retorts in his booming voice as she walks out. "Maybe, this time, we'll get through security with more than an hour until our flight takes off."

It sounds like she says, "That's pointless," and I snicker at their banter even though I'm not sure while my father kisses my cheek before following right behind her.

Then, I'm all alone at eight on a Friday night. The boys are asleep, although Landon has occasional nights where he'll wake up a few times, and the chances of my parents coming back downstairs tonight are slim.

Sure, they are all in the house, less than a minute away if I need them. Irrelevant, however, since that's not the type of alone I'm talking about.

With the exception of that one night, Oliver and I were together for over twelve years. Best friends, then lovers, and finally, parents. For a long time, we were all each other had. That slowly changed after we got married, both of us cultivating and maintaining friendships with others — he from work while I became friends with a few other mothers from play groups.

Having a child really helped bring me out of my own shell and going out to dinner with Oliver's co-workers who were married with children as well meant we were kept busy with one dinner party or get together, such as a birthday party, after another.

And through all the spreading our wings and gaining new friends, we always made time for just us. Even if we did nothing more than hire a babysitter to go out to dinner and dance.

Yes, he had been shocked I wanted to learn to dance, but we were as great at dancing as we had been in my dream once we got the hang of it. It brought us closer together even as we became more of our own selves and let go of the dependency we had on each other.

So being alone? I haven't been alone in a long time and don't know what the hell to do. Do I need him to breathe? No. To live? No...but I never thought I'd have to live without him, either.

I think of him when watching TV, eating at the kitchen table, and standing on the back porch watching Wyatt run around the yard. I miss him, and every bit of this house is a reminder of the fact he's never coming back.

At first, I thought about selling the house and finding somewhere else for us to live because the pain had been unbearable. Even had a couple interested buyers, but in the end, I couldn't do it.

For eight months, none of his things were touched except when cleaning the house. The mere idea of putting his things into boxes to store and perhaps get rid of one day had been too much to process or deal with.

Today, though...today had been different. I woke up, saw his pants stacked on top of the dresser — where they had been for over half a year — and for once, hadn't cried at the sight of them.

Instead, I got out of the bed, walked over to the dresser, picked the stack up, and then angrily threw them one-by-one across the room. Then, I headed over to the closet and started grabbing his stuff to get it the hell out of there.

By the time my mother came in to see what all

the noise had been about, his things were all over the floor, and I sat among them sobbing my eyes out while clutching one of his shirts to my chest.

I kept that shirt. The rest of his things are now in boxes, and before I wake in the morning, my father will have placed them all in the attic before leaving for the airport.

Not because I want to get rid of him, but because they are Oliver's and I don't want a repeat of this morning. He's in my heart, he's half of our children, and he's all over this house in my memories.

There's no forgetting him even as I attempt to move forward with my life.

Tomorrow.

I'll definitely move forward tomorrow.

As for tonight?

I turn off the lights and head upstairs to our room, change into my tank and shorts before slipping my arms into the sleeves of the shirt that still smells like him, and climb into bed.

One more night of pretending that he's okay, and he'll be home soon to wrap me in his arms as we sleep before I wake up and face life without him once more.

TURNS OUT HANDLING TWO KIDS ON MY OWN IS a lot harder than I thought it would be. My parents helping meant me being alone with both boys at the same time hasn't happened, but I'm determined to do it because I have to.

They've been gone a week, and I will not call them, no matter how overwhelmed I am.

However, after two attempts to shop with Wyatt and Landon in tow — Wyatt threw fits in his seat when I wouldn't get him something he wanted which prompted Landon to join in by crying in my ear from his perch on my hip — I give up and call the babysitter so I can get groceries in peace.

And I'm standing in the bread aisle, about to head to the checkouts, when *he* asks from behind me, "Darcy?"

I haven't heard Zach's voice since the hospital. Every now and then we saw each other in public, acknowledged it with a nod, and went our separate ways.

Guess he doesn't think we need to not speak anymore.

Turning, I don't even bother smiling, choosing to meet his uncertain expression with a blank one as I noticed he hasn't physically changed one damn bit. "Zach."

Hesitancy disappearing, his words are warm and caring as he says, "I heard about Oliver. I'm sorry for your loss doesn't seem adequate at this moment."

"It isn't," I assure him while sticking the loaf of bread in the front seat. "No need to say it, however. I've heard it enough to last me a lifetime."

He nods and it hurts to look at the affection in his eyes, so I focus on where my hands grip the cart, reminding myself of the day in the store with a moment like this all those years ago.

In my peripheral vision, he steps closer and places his hand on top of mine on the cart in silence.

"I've wanted to call every day to see how you were doing. I didn't because hearing from me seemed like the last thing you would want."

I barely refrain from yanking away from his touch as his words cause the corner of my eyes to prickle with tears begging to get out. "Good decision. Standing here with you right now is hard enough."

His sharp intake of breath is impossible to miss, his hand leaving mine simultaneously as he clears his throat and steps back. "Sorry to bother you. I wanted nothing but to see how you were doing."

I feel like a bitch as he goes to walk away and stop him by reaching to grab his bare arm. "Zach—"

Only whatever I was going to say sticks in my

throat and dies at the heat in his glare. His hair, his eyes...and god, his entire face.

His gaze is burning into mine, yet it's my hand I jerk back as if his skin has scorched mine while my stomach rolls and my mouth goes dry.

Why hadn't I seen it before?

And how the hell could I have been so blind?

I can't see my own face, but I know the color's drained out of it, especially when he asks with concern, "What's wrong?"

"Everything." My entire body grows cold, my hands beginning to shake, and right now I can't do anything except get away from him until I can straighten out the thoughts in my head. "I've...I've gotta go. I'm sorry for being rude. I just..."

Not even saying goodbye, I push the cart, holding my breath the whole time in hope he won't come after me because if he does, I'm going to start bawling.

Thankfully, he doesn't, but I only make it to the car before breaking down, sick from the encounter and everything it might mean for me.

No matter how great our life turned out or how much both Oliver and I grew together during our relationship, there's one potentially huge mistake made I can no longer ignore.

I never considered the fact pregnancy might have resulted from my little interlude with Zach. After all, he deliberately pulled out to avoid that specific outcome and pointed it out as a way to insult me.

But I'm not naive and never have been. I should've questioned it because of the timing, yet didn't. Hell, none of us did. Well, I don't know about Oliver; if he ever had doubts, he never said a word to me.

Wyatt, our now four-year-old son, had been born with strawberry blond hair. His newborn blue eyes changed to the green of mine later on while his hair has progressively lightened over the years.

Early on, we both figured he took after me, and it really never entered my mind to consider another possibility because I was convinced he was Oliver's child.

Yet, one look at our eight-month-old, with his dark hair and dark eyes so like his father, and I'm afraid the truth is right here in front of my eyes as it has been all along.

When Landon was five months old, my mother innocently pointed out how different the boys were from each other as she presented a photo of my grandfather when he was a child — and Wyatt does resemble him quite a bit.

Because of that, I had put it out of my mind without another thought.

Neither of my parents knows anything about the incidences with Zach, and it will be hard to explain to them if my suspicions are confirmed.

However, after running into him at the store, the differences between Wyatt and Landon became too much to disregard any longer.

I need to know for certain before saying something, so a few days after seeing Zach, I had a private DNA test performed on the children and myself to determine whether they are half or full siblings.

And now, nearly three weeks later, the results have finally arrived.

What do I want them to be?

Staring down at the envelope clenched in my grasp, that's the main question running through my mind since one of the answers will change me and my son's lives forever.

If he is Zach's, I'll have to tell him, and he'll be in my life from that day forward in a way neither of us can run away from.

Who knows how he'll react. With our history, I'm afraid he'll think I did it on purpose and having to deal with that raises my anxiety. Plus, the idea of having to see him, talk to him, and co-parent with him after all this time is enough to make me want to burn this envelope without even looking.

But the urge passes in a second because even taking into account everything between the two of us, I'm not the type of woman to do such a thing and deny a father a relationship with his child.

After taking a deep breath and letting it out slowly, I slide my finger under the flap and prepare to find out the results as I grab the paper from inside.

Two seconds to unfold the paper and another ten to skim the most important information before the paper drifts to the floor at my sharp gasp.

Wyatt and Landon are half-siblings.

Wyatt is Zach's son.

Now, for the second time in a year, our lives have changed forever, and nothing will ever be the same.

PART III
WHAT WILL BE

Not thinking about Darcy and wondering how she's holding up is impossible.

The thoughts of her are so pervasive they are distracting enough to prevent me getting any work done.

God, the moment I spotted her in the store earlier today, I wanted to walk up and wrap her in my arms. Even in her noticeably depressed and exhausted state, she looked beautiful.

I spotted her a few times over the years for brief moments; she'd always been alone. Never did anything more than nod in her direction as a greeting and I nearly passed her by earlier today without saying anything out of habit. A healthy dose of worry at approaching her after we shut the door on our past five years ago had me second guessing my decision as well.

Hard to believe it has been that long. Hell, hard to wrap my head around Oliver dying in such a gruesome way. The shooting at his work had been all over the news, and although I hadn't known the guy, Darcy loved him. Her grief earlier had been palpable, as if she's barely holding it together, and there's no doubt I would feel the same if it had happened to someone I love.

Is it appropriate to want to ease her suffering in any way I can? I don't know, and it hadn't helped as she stood there stating that being near me caused her more pain.

And her expression, when I asked her what was wrong, killed me. "Everything," she had said, her whole face going white as if she'd looked into my face and felt sick, or suddenly saw a fucking ghost.

I hadn't followed when she rushed away, gutted at the way she couldn't wait to get away from me, but now I regret it. Reaching out to her may backfire — if she hadn't wanted to talk at the store, she might not want to speak to me at all — so I'm going to give it a bit more time before attempting to talk to her again.

She's never been one to ask for help and might need support. We may not be friends, and our past is a little ugly, but I've always cared about her. Hell, who am I kidding? I loved her and still feel more for her than I want to admit out loud. I can't tell her that, but I do want her to know I'm here for her.

In the meantime, however, I need to get some damn work done, so opening my calendar, I set a reminder a month from now to get in touch with her. Not because I'll forget, but because writing it down helps me push thoughts about her aside for now.

Then, hard as it is, I do just that and get back to the important paperwork stacked in a pile on my desk.

"Daddy, I'm starving."

Glancing up from where I'm preparing food for us, my forever dramatic almost eight-year-old daughter stands in the open kitchen doorway wearing a sundress and tennis shoes with mismatched socks.

Shoes she has on the wrong feet; something she gets right about fifty-percent of the time. It's adorable and frustrating all at once, as we've discussed the way to ensure her shoes go on properly many times, but the information hasn't stuck in her brain yet.

"Lunch is almost ready," I reply with a pointed look at her feet. "Fix your shoes, sweetheart."

Rose peeks at her feet and lets out a sigh, her whole face turning pink as she says, "Oh, I got it wrong again. I'm stupid."

"Hey, we don't call ourselves names. You're not stupid."

"Jessica said I was." She stomps over to the table and takes a seat in the chair before pulling off her shoes. "She said only babies or stupid dummies don't know how to put their shoes on right."

God, even if she's only a second grader, this little Jessica girl pisses me off. It isn't the first time she's spouted bullshit at Rose, but my patience with the whole situation is running thin since it doesn't seem her parents are taking care of the problem.

"Jessica is wrong. Period." Picking up the plates with our sandwiches, I carry them over to the table and then get us some water before sitting across from her as she finishes fixing her shoes. "I know it's hard not to listen to her, but you aren't any of those things. Everyone is different."

"Okay."

She mumbles the word, not believing me, and to make her feel better I scoot back my chair to kick off my shoes.

Her eyes round as I lean over. "What are you doing, Daddy?"

"I'm fixing my shoes. I think I have them on the

wrong feet." I slip my feet back into the shoes so they're on wrong and lift them up toward her for inspection. "There. Much better."

She bites her lip, her eyes tearing up a little before she straightens her shoulders and giggles at me. "No, they're wrong, Daddy. See?" She points to the toe area. "The big parts should be touching."

"Oh, damn, you're right." After fixing them again, I sit up in the chair only to find her wiping a tear from her cheek and her lower lip wobbling. "Why are you crying?"

"It's not fair."

"What isn't?"

She sits back on the chair and sticks her feet straight out. "I can't see the bottom of my feet to tell my shoes are wrong like this."

We're both silent for a moment and then, her sudden howls of laughter are followed by mine.

Crisis averted for now.

And later, I'll send an email to my daughter's principal to see what can be done about that little troublemaker Jessica.

ROSE'S PIGTAILS FLY BEHIND HER AS SHE rushes into the living room, tosses her book bag on the chair, and declares with a huge smile, "Jessica wasn't mean to me today!"

"I'm glad, sweetheart." And after my note to the principal, I doubt she ever will be again. "Hopefully she learned her lesson about being mean to others and will be nicer."

"Yeah." She gets on the couch and takes a seat next to me, her expression brightening even more as she says, "At recess, she said sorry, and I told her it was okay. Then I shared with her at snack time; she didn't have one today."

"That was kind of you."

Her entire expression is serious as she nods at me before leaning into my side. "I think she needs a friend, Daddy, so I told her we can be friends if she wants 'cause I need friends."

God, she's so good-natured. Sometimes I wonder where she gets it from, then realize she's never experienced the less kind side of me, and I don't plan on ever letting her see it. Wrapping my arm around her shoulder, I hug her to my side and smile. "Did she accept?"

"Yep! And I asked her if she wanted to come to my house and play one day and she said yes. Can she?"

"If you want." I'm not certain I want a kid who tortured mine for the first two months of school in my house but if my daughter's giving the girl a chance, then so will I. "On Monday, you can give her our number and tell her to ask her parents to call me."

"Thank you, Daddy!" Moving fast, she wraps her arms around my neck and kisses my cheek, drawing away before I can reciprocate to slide off the couch. "I'm going outside to play."

"No homework?"

She nods and crosses her arm over her chest with a cute pout. "I don't want to do it right now."

This is most when she's like me. I did well in school, but hated homework, finding many ways to avoid doing it. And although she has to do it just as I had to, I don't feel like giving her the homework is important speech tonight, even though I don't think that's true at all.

Ah, parenthood — telling your child fibs to get them to do things you don't even want to do yourself to prepare them for adulthood.

Having just gotten home from school, however, I'm more than happy to give her a break and have a little fun.

"One hour," I tell her in my serious tone so she knows there will be no arguments about this. "Then, come inside and do your homework before dinner."

"Okay!" She beams at me and skips off toward with the back door.

Easy.

Too easy.

I know in a few years, I'll be looking back at her this age and wish for her back. She's sweet now but has moments where her mood shifts from happy to downright petulant in a matter of seconds, especially when she doesn't get her way.

Never have given into her fits, yet it doesn't stop her from trying repeatedly. I can't imagine what it will be like when she's a teenager, as my experience with teenage girls is limited to my teen years, and going by that...well, it makes me want to lock her up in her room as a pre-emptive measure.

Rose's voice carries through the open windows while she sings at the top of her lungs from where she plays in the backyard, distracting me from my thoughts just as my phone dings.

Call Darcy.

I stare at the banner on the locked screen, swipe my finger across it, and tap on her name in my contacts. Hoping the number is the correct one — I only found one in my search, under her husband's name — I press the phone icon and put the phone up to my ear while holding my breath.

When the automated message announces the

number is no longer in order, there's nothing I can do except go see her in person if I want to see how she's doing.

And that's exactly what I'm going to do as soon as possible because I'm done waiting.

"I'm jumping! Look, I'm jumping!"

As much as Wyatt attempts to get me to turn around, I don't and simply say, "I know you're not jumping on the couch, because you're not supposed to, and you don't want to go in time out, do you?"

Bingo. He doesn't answer me and the occasional squeaking suddenly stops.

A second later, he comes up to the computer and rubs my arm, his eyes bright as he gives me a cheeky smile and begins jumping again when I look at him.

Sighing, I shut off the monitor and move my chair back gently, turning the seat to face him as he stops jumping and continues to grin at me.

Of course, he does. He got what he wanted —

my undivided attention since his brother is sleeping.

Then, he climbs into my lap and snuggles against my chest. Wrapping my arms around his little body, I rest my chin on the top of his head and sigh as he relaxes into me. "Okay, buddy, what do you want to do?"

"Jump," he mumbles, sounding more like he needs a nap than anything else.

Standing up, I grab the baby monitor, carry him to my bedroom and place him on the bed before placing the monitor on the nightstand and crawling in next to him because I'm tired, too.

I haven't slept well since learning the little boy cuddling against me and sighing with contentment is Zach's, a revelation that changes everything and leaves me with nothing to do except tell Zach.

Pretty much the only thing I've thought about for two weeks now and still haven't done what I should do because standing close to him in the store had been difficult enough. How will I handle having him in my life and my boys' life after our history together and losing Oliver, who was Daddy to Wyatt and is the one he misses and cries for?

I wonder how I can introduce a new man into my son's life so soon, and yet, how can I avoid it under the circumstances? The longer I put off telling him, the worse Zach's reaction might be since their similarities are obvious.

As for my parents, I don't look forward to making them aware of what's going on when they return in two weeks and have considered not telling Zach until I talk to them.

But, like all things lately, I don't know what to do or how to do it. I'm lost, tired, and frustrated with this whole situation making my life a little harder than it already has been since Oliver died.

And I'm not even going to get some rest even though Wyatt's fast asleep in my arms as Landon's soft cries beg for my attention the moment I shut my eyes.

Sighing, I move slow and easy away from Wyatt to avoid waking him before heading to Landon's room just down the hall, and put all my attention on him instead of the major encounter ahead of me I don't get to avoid no matter my preference.

ANOTHER WEEK HAS PASSED BY WITHOUT ME telling Zach.

I think it's worse because this is something that I have to tell him in person and the idea of seeing him brings up all these feelings I want to flat out ignore.

Pushed aside not once, but twice, those same emotions and the attraction between us won't be shoved away again. I hadn't wanted to admit it to myself at the time, yet it's why standing there with him had been so difficult.

Everything is still there between us, and the anger I had directed at him should've been directed at myself because I'm the one with a problem.

Oliver's been dead less than a year; how can I possibly want anyone else or even think about another man in that way? We may not have started off being the most passionate couple, but by the end, our entire relationship had changed.

We had been like the us from the dream I'm not positive was a dream even to this day. After it, though, I became the best wife and mother I could be and loved my husband with everything I had.

In the store, Zach touched me, and I had wanted his comfort with a need I can't consider anything other than inappropriate at this time in my life.

What will happen if I see him? He's always been able to read me. The day in the bookstore, I gave him what he wanted because I had wanted it too. Seeing him after all that time, there had been no avoiding it, no matter the lies I told myself before then.

I won't lie now, however. Whatever is between us, though, we shouldn't open the door on it, not when we were able to finally shut it peacefully that day in the hospital.

But there is a little boy who is half of each of us, and I have to do the right thing, even if I have to find a way for us to have as little contact as possible while ensuring Zach knows his son.

Sighing, because this is giving me a headache, I pour a glass of wine and head to the living room to spend another Friday night alone watching shows on Netflix like I used to with Oliver. Not every Friday, but a lot of them.

Just as I'm about to settle in to watch a comedy show in hopes a little laughter will cheer me up when the doorbell rings.

Unsure of who the hell I know that would be here at eight-thirty on a Friday night, I set down the wine and place it on the table before going to answer.

The last thing I expect to see is Zach's face through the peephole and immediately want not to answer it. He'll go away eventually, right? But if he keeps ringing the doorbell, he might wake up the boys, and that will ruin my plan on going to bed early to get some rest.

Taking a deep breath, I let it out slowly and then paste a smile on my face before opening the door. "Zach, what are you doing here?"

"Not wasting any time on pleasantries, huh?" He grins as my face flushes in uncontrollable embarrassment when I realize how rude I'm being and nods at the foyer behind me. "Mind if I come in for a few minutes? Unless this isn't a good time."

I step back before thinking about why he would want to come inside, and he walks past me, whistling. After I shut the door, he turns to face me and crosses his arms over his chest. "I tried to call to see how you are doing, but the only number I could find was disconnected."

"So you decided a Friday night was the perfect time to come over."

"Yes. Well, no, not exactly."

Thinking he'll elaborate, I wait, only he doesn't. Instead, he turns away and strides further inside the house, leaving me to trail after him with any protest stuck in my throat. This isn't how I wanted him to find out about Wyatt, and if he catches sight of the photos, it will be impossible to deny.

He leads us into the living room and sits down in the recliner — Oliver's favorite chair. Nobody except Wyatt has sat in it, and without even thinking about how seeing him sitting there makes me feel, I shove his arm from where I've stopped beside him.

"Get out of there. You can't sit there." He lifts a brow at me while resting his arms at his sides and I point back toward the front door. "You have to leave. I'll... I'll call you."

He studies my face, lifting a hand to rub his jaw before glancing around the room and then back at me while ignoring my demand that he leaves. "Why can't I sit here? Oliver sat in more than this chair, didn't he?"

Yes, he did, but the way Zach is acting ticks me off. "Get up," I hiss at him, slapping at his arm and not caring this is probably a pretty childish way to respond to whatever the hell he's doing. "I don't want you in that chair or this house!"

"Ouch." He snatches the hand hitting him and holds it tight while rising from the seat, tugging on it until our bodies are touching while my breathing hangs harsh between us. "No need for this, Darcy. I just want to talk."

I refuse to look at him and avert my gaze toward the fireplace, hoping he cares more about getting me to focus on him than checking out the pictures on the mantle. "About what? You can see I'm fine. Me and the boys, we're good. And you need to go."

"I see that. And you're beautiful." His compliment is hushed as he leans in to press a kiss to my temple, making my body tremble despite itself, deprived too long of affection from anyone except the boys. "Always knew motherhood would look good on you."

And in this exact moment where I can feel the effect us being this close is having on him, the one thing I haven't been ready to tell him about arrives in the room with a softly spoken, "Mommy?"

Zach freezes, his whole body going rigid as his grip tightens on my hand to the point of painful as he sees exactly what I didn't want him to yet; what I knew he would see the instant he caught sight of Wyatt.

He releases me gently after hissing, "What the hell, Darcy?"

Unable to meet his gaze, knowing it will be filled with fury and questions, I take a step back and whisper, "Give me a few minutes and I'll...I'll be right back."

"Oh, I'll be waiting."

Whirling around at his statement filled with suppressed fury, I head over to Wyatt, pick him up and my arms, and carry him back to the bedroom as he asks the one question I'm not ready to answer.

"Mommy, who is that man?"

ZACHARY

"He's mine, isn't he?"

Darcy's barely returned to the room after being gone ten minutes when I ask her the question, and she takes her damn time answering it.

Not that it matters, as I knew the moment the little boy tried to get her attention from the doorway and stared right at me with his thumb jammed in his mouth. He could've been me as a kid, for fuck's sake.

But, why the hell wouldn't she tell me?

She sighs from where she stands by the fireplace and grabs a picture before turning to me with watery eyes, her expression harboring the same devastation filling my chest.

"I didn't know," she finally croaks after a few moments of staring down at the photo clutched in her hands. "That is until I saw you in the store and realized it might be possible."

Ah. "That explains your reaction."

"Yes." She walks closer, stopping about a foot from where I stand, and holds up the photo for me to take. "I did a test between the boys and..." She swallows, her eyes wracked with guilt as she finally meets my gaze. "Wyatt's yours. I was trying to find a way to tell you."

Hard not to be pissed, even though her sincerity in not knowing is plain to see, and I frown while staring down at a baby photo of my son. "How could you not know all these years, Darcy?"

"I guess Oliver and I just saw what we wanted to. We chalked his looks up to taking after me, which he does, a lot. And none of us ever questioned it. I mean, you knew I was pregnant. It's not like any of us thought about the timing of it." She steps back, grabbing a tissue from the coffee table and blowing into it before continuing. "And you pulled out. What was I to think? I know it can happen, but it didn't even dawn on me at the time."

Dammit, she's right. Other than thinking about those moments with her for other reasons, none of those included thinking she might have gotten pregnant from it. She married Oliver, and I trusted the baby was his without a doubt.

"Wow." Shoving a hand through my hair, I

move to the couch and take a seat, my eyes glued to the picture as I mutter, "Fuck, we were stupid."

She lets out a little laugh, one that is quickly followed by a sharp inhale, and I glance up to find her standing in front of me with tears streaming down her face as she breaks down into sobs.

"I'm s-sorry," she wails and hides her face in her hands as her shoulders shake. "I should've thought...I can't..."

Setting aside the picture, I reach out and take her into my arms, unable to watch her break down in front of me without comforting her.

"Shh. Don't cry, Darcy. I'm not angry."

It's the truth. I'm not mad. Perhaps I should be since I've lost out on over four years of my son's life that I wouldn't have if I had known all this time, even if she were married to Oliver. However, that's both our faults, for ignoring the potential repercussions of our actions while trying to deal with our past issues.

She curls into me, crying harder at my words, and leaving me helpless to do anything except hold her close.

I also understand her breakdown has nothing to do with me.

Yes, my entire night has gone differently than I imagined it, and my life is once again changed forever with this revelation. Shocked and elated simultaneously, I'm wondering how the hell we're going to co-parent our son who doesn't even know who the fuck I am.

But Darcy lost her husband and found out her oldest child belongs to another man. She has a child with *me*, after everything between us, which means we're tied together forever despite the way we managed to cut the binds from before.

We share a past, and now, a present along with a future neither of us can ignore because we have a child who needs us both in his life.

And even if Darcy won't admit it, she needs me right now, too.

So I'll sit here and let her cry for as long as necessary because as of this moment, we've got plenty of time to figure things out.

WHEN SHE FINALLY SITS UP, I HAVE NO IDEA how much time has passed, but her eyes are brighter and less sad than when I arrived.

Grabbing her a tissue, she wipes her eyes and her face, then crumples it in her hand and blushes as the fact she's straddling my lap registers.

She slides off to sit beside me and clears her throat while meeting my gaze with a hesitant lift of her lips. "Thank you. I've been so worried you would be angry at me; I wasn't prepared for anything else."

Reaching over, I grab her hand and squeeze to reassure her. "I'm not an asshole, Darcy. I care about what's best for our son, and that's it. Anger is useless here."

She nods and tugs her hand out from under mine before standing up. "Honestly, I don't know what to do. I mean, what do we do? Wyatt's only four, but Oliver was his daddy. He doesn't know you and he won't understand."

"Don't make yourself sick over it. Those are all completely understandable fears." Rising as well, I step closer to her and place my hands on her shoulders, waiting until she meets my gaze to speak. "We'll start slow. For now, I'm your friend, and we're all going to spend time together having fun. That's all you have to tell him. Everything else, we'll work out later."

She swallows hard, her eyes searching mine. "I'll have to tell my parents."

Not what I expected her to say. "What?"

"My parents. I reconciled with them while pregnant with Wyatt. They've been helping out since Oliver died and will be back soon from their trip. They don't know yet."

Shit. Her parents never liked me. And for the longest time, I hated them for the ultimatum they gave her that changed our lives. The last thing I want is to deal with them.

But Darcy must know what I'm thinking because she laughs softly and shakes her head. "Don't worry, Zach. They're not anything like they were back then. All this may shock them, but we're all adults here."

Blowing out the breath I hadn't realized I was holding, I drop my hands from her shoulders with a nod. "If you've forgiven them, then so can I. Difficult sometimes, having moments where everything feels as if it happened yesterday, not fifteen years ago."

"I know!" She laughs and moves across the room, tossing the tissue in the tiny trash can before turning to me with a curious expression. "How's Rose doing?"

"She's great. We were having some issues with another girl in her class, but everything is good now." I glance at my watch. "Shit. I need to get back; wasn't planning on being gone this long."

"Oh, okay. Sure."

Her tone and expression are neutral, but I get the feeling she's disappointed.

Or maybe that's just my hope. Either way, I ignore it and say, "We should exchange numbers. We can work out what to do next another time."

Agreeing, she pulls out her phone, and after

that's finished, she walks with me to the front door, her hands behind her back the whole way.

Because she's not expecting it, and I can't resist, I pull her into a hug after opening the front door. She doesn't resist it long, reciprocating by slipping her arms around my waist, and relaxing into my hold with a sigh.

I kiss the top of her head and smile at the way she stiffens a little in my embrace from the unexpected affection even as her breath hitches. "I'll call you in a few days."

"Sure." She draws away and avoids looking me in the face as she steps back and grabs the door handle. "See you later."

The door shuts behind me with a soft click, and after I hear the lock slide into place, I head toward the car with a grin on my face.

Seeing her hadn't gone at all as I expected, but having a son with Darcy makes me wonder what else will happen, and if this is the start of a second chance I've spent years believing we would never get.

"Hm." My mother sits back and takes a sip of her coffee, her reaction surprisingly underwhelming considering what I've just told her.

My father doesn't say anything at all. He sits next to my mother with his chin resting on his hand and does nothing except stare at me thoughtfully.

Almost makes me want to fidget in my seat like a teenager in trouble because I can't tell what they're thinking.

Not that it should matter because Wyatt is Zach's and he will be coming around to spend time with our son.

I've had to practice saying those words in my head and to accept them as the truth they are just to be able to say it out loud.

Finally, my mother sets down her cup, purses

her lips, and then asks the one thing I should've known she would. "Is there a chance of you two rekindling your relationship?"

"No," I respond instantly along with a huff. "My god, that hasn't even crossed my mind."

"Perhaps not yours," my father says, chuckling. "But what about him?"

My mother nods in agreement. "You two have a history, apparently even more than your father and I knew of. It isn't impossible, darling."

Unbelievable.

My parents are the last people I would imagine wanting me to give Zach a second chance.

I truly haven't thought about it except briefly and decided it wouldn't be good for either of us to go that direction.

We have Wyatt to think of, to take care of. We can't mess that up by trying to date again and seeing if things work out, can we? No. We're in a good place, and we should stay there for the sake of our son. Anything else is just asking for trouble.

"It won't happen," I assure them, standing up as Landon's hungry cries pierce the silence through the tiny baby monitor. "And that's my cue to get away from this absurd conversation."

Their eyes are on me as I walk away and my mother's laughing comment follows me as I turn the corner. "It really isn't that ridiculous of a thought."

Perhaps the idea isn't, but it is one I'm not going to entertain for even a moment.

In fact, I'm going to flat out ignore it, and hope Zach hasn't gotten the same idea as my parents because I don't want anything more than to be friends again.

A whole week has passed since my parents returned and although Zach asked how the discussion went, I didn't tell him anything beyond their awareness of what's going on.

He definitely tries to get me to talk to him. Every single day he texts me to say good morning, asks how I am in the afternoon, and says to tell Wyatt good night for him.

I haven't, since Wyatt doesn't know who he is, but that will change today when he comes to visit after lunch.

Zach decided he wants to wait to tell Rose about Wyatt and that means in order to spend time with him without leaving Rose with a babysitter is for him to visit during school hours.

Tried not to think about how this makes me feel better since coming in the middle of the day will keep him from running into my parents — both busy with their charity and related activities — and will leave us with no alone time thanks to the children.

Not that I'm worried about being alone with him.

Okay, that's a bit of a lie.

I had been okay with hugging him, believing it nothing more than a friendly gesture, but the kisses from him really threw me.

And the way he took the news about Wyatt shocked me. I expected the Zach from five years ago — the one who considered me no different from our teen years and might think I lied about not knowing. Yet, he hadn't.

Plus, the way he smiled and gazed at me was like the Zach who used to love me. I haven't experienced that since I was sixteen and broke his heart, which is definitely something I don't want a repeat of.

So if he does have the same idea as my parents, I'm going to have to nip it pretty quick, and hope doing that won't make things awkward between us.

Glancing at the clock as the doorbell rings to see Zach is right on time, I pick up Landon and perch him on my hip before heading toward the front door.

He greets me with a bright smile, hands in his jean pockets as he stands on the porch. "Hey."

"Hey. Come on in." I step back and let him pass through, then shut the door. "Wyatt's in the living room playing with the big legos, building his version of a castle apparently."

"Nice." His eyes move from my face to Landon, who stares at him with curiosity while chewing on his fingers. "Hey, buddy."

Landon's eyes go wide. He only stares at Zach for a moment before shoving his face into my shoulder and wrapping his free hand around my neck.

Zach laughs and looks at me once again. "Shy is his middle name?"

"Yep." Rubbing Landon's back, I step away and nod toward the living room. "Follow me."

As we head that way, Zach is a step behind me, and when Landon giggles, I glance back over my shoulder to find Zach making a silly face.

He winks at me, relaxing his expression as we step into the living room, where Wyatt looks up at us only to freeze mid-play.

Then, he points at Zach and states, "That man," making it evident he remembers him from the night he walked in on us.

"Hey, there," Zach says without missing a beat,

walking over to sit next to our son on the floor. "I'm your mommy's friend. Can I play, too?"

Wyatt doesn't even blink; just accepts Zach's explanation with a nod and goes back to building, all while I marvel at the way they look so damn alike. They even have the same slight head tilt to the left side when they concentrate.

I truly had been in denial all these years.

Landon starts fussing because he's hungry and I leave Zach playing with Wyatt while heading to Landon's room to feed him. I don't usually bother, but the idea of breastfeeding in front of Zach makes me a little uncomfortable, and at least in his room, there is a comfy chair, unlike in the kitchen.

Sitting down with a sigh, he latches on with a happy sound, then eats while I rock us back and forth gently. The food plus the rocking eventually lulls Landon into a nap, and when my own eyes beg to close for just a few moments, I recline the chair and give in to temptation for a little rest.

AT THE TOUCH OF A HAND ON MY SHOULDER, I jerk awake to empty arms and my chest covered up by my dress once again while Zach stands over me.

He brings one finger up to his smirking lips and

turns to the side, pointing at the crib where Landon sleeps peacefully in the darkening room.

Rising from the chair, I follow him out of the bedroom and leave the door cracked a little before heading toward the kitchen for some water.

When I enter, Wyatt's at the table eating a fruit bar and waves at me after taking a drink of his milk. "Hi, Mommy! I want you to see the big castle we built!"

"After you finish eating, sweetie," I say to him, only to glance at the clock, and wince at the fact nearly two hours have passed since Zach arrived. He stands nearby, his arms over his chest while watching me, as I drink from the bottle of water. "I didn't mean to fall asleep. I'm sure you didn't plan on being there this long."

He shrugs. "I didn't, but no big deal. Figured you needed the sleep, and we had fun, didn't we, Wyatt?"

"Yep! I want to build another castle. A huger one."

"Next time, buddy." Taking a step closer, he puts his hand on the small of my back and smiles at our son. "Your mom is going to show me out and then she'll come back to see the castle, okay?"

"Okay!"

We're all the way by the front door before he speaks again.

"Thanks for today. Think we can do it again the same time next week?"

"Uh, sure." My face flushes at the smile on his face, realizing he had to have fixed my clothing when he moved Landon to his bed and doing my best not to focus on it. "I'll try not to fall asleep next time."

"No worries." He lifts a hand to my face and cups it, ignoring my sharp intake of breath as he leans in to press a kiss to the side of my lips before drawing away with a bigger grin and a mischievous gleam in his eyes. "I came in earlier, and you looked so peaceful, I couldn't wake you. Feeling refreshed, at least?"

"Y-yeah." I step back, attempting to get away from the look in his eyes and the way his kiss and touch make me want things I've decided not to have... especially because he definitely fixed my clothing while I slept. "Thank you for letting me sleep when you didn't have to. Hopefully, it doesn't mess up your day too much."

His hands slide back into his pockets as they were on his arrival. "Nah. I took the day off. And you're welcome."

"So, next week?"

"Yep. I'll call you if anything changes."

"Great."

He opens the door and steps through only to

look back at me with a question in his eyes. But when I ask, "What?" he merely shakes his head and says, "Nothing."

Then, he strides toward his truck without looking back and drives away with a little wave.

For the rest of the evening, I wondered what he wanted to ask but didn't, and whether my answer would be the one he desired.

Then, I remind myself I shouldn't care, and resolve to make sure he knows where the boundaries are from now on.

Darcy sits next to me on the bench at the park, her eyes concentrated on where Landon plays in the sandbox nearby while Wyatt enjoys the slide and Rose squeals with delight while making her swing go higher and higher.

After three visits to her house to spend time with Wyatt, I decided it was time to tell Rose she has a brother, and yesterday told her everything I could that was age appropriate. It was more complicated than I thought, trying to explain how I have a son and she has a brother I didn't know about but told her a mistake was made and left it at that. I also told her Wyatt is too young to understand, so we were just going to be his and his mommy's friends.

Usually, she questions a lot of things, so it was

a relief when she accepted my explanation before asking when she would get to meet him. And nothing makes me happier than how accepting she is, as she immediately began making plans for how she and her brother will spend their time together.

The park today was her idea, for example.

I hated giving Darcy such short notice but she took it in stride and now here we are. We introduced the kids, and it had been amusing the way they both began trying to talk each other's ear off as they played. It hadn't taken long for the whole situation to ease into them alternating between doing their own thing and having fun together.

Darcy, on the other hand, hasn't looked my way much and I'm positive her refusal to do so is my fault even though I don't know what I did.

After the first visit, things became awkward between us, and I haven't known what to say to make it better. She wanders off with Landon after I arrive and reappears when it is time for me to leave, Landon perched on her hip, and gives short, clipped responses to my texts, not talking to me much beyond when discussing Wyatt.

It has gone on long enough that I want an answer and now is as good a time as any.

"Why don't you tell me what I did," I say while

scooting a bit closer to her, until our knees touch, "so this awkwardness between us will go away."

Her gaze remains on Landon as she says, "You didn't do anything."

"I did something, Darcy. You won't even look at me. Not just today, but since my first visit to see Wyatt."

"You didn't do anything," she repeats with a shrug. "Things are better this way."

"How so?"

"Our focus needs to be on Wyatt and doing what's best for him. At my place, you're there to spend time with him. I have nothing to do with it."

Wrong. "How things are between us is important, which means you've got everything to do with it, sweetheart."

She stiffens and shoots me a glare, then quickly realizes what she's doing and jerks her gaze away. "Don't call me that."

Nothing like seeing a spark in her eyes to thrill me. She's hard to read sometimes, but something is really bothering her, and I won't let it go until she gives in. "Come on. Tell me what's wrong."

I fear she won't answer me until she huffs, her voice overflowing with emotion as she says, "One of the things I worried about when thinking how to tell you about Wyatt was the impact it would have on my life. We ended anything between us years ago, and now I would have to see you and have you in my life, whether I wanted it or not. And after everything? I don't, not in the slightest."

Not surprised, although her words sting. "Darcy—"

She holds up a hand and finally turns to face me, her eyes glistening with tears. "My life has been turned upside down enough with Oliver dying and the truth about our...our son. Right now, I am doing the best I can, and this is all I can give you. You're invading my life as it is and I don't need you or my parents getting any ideas."

A little guilt creeps in because I do have hopes of things turning romantic between us again, but I can't resist chuckling at the end of her statement. "Your parents?"

She isn't amused and glares at me again. "Yes. They think since you obviously got close enough to get me pregnant five years ago that something more now might be possible. I assured them it isn't."

Damn. Her parents are on the same side as me. Hell has definitely frozen over. "Perhaps speaking in absolutes is something we should avoid. Moments before you spotted me in the bookstore, I have no doubt we were both positive seeing each other again would never happen for the rest of our lives."

Her gaze dances away as she bites her lip, the

action making me want to put my mouth on hers, and after she peeks a glimpse of all the kids, she looks at me again while shaking her head. "Doesn't matter. Things were different then."

"Of course they are. Things change. Saying with absolute certainty that nothing will happen between us is foolish, however."

Oh, she doesn't like that. The glower is back. "Zach—"

"Darcy." I cover her hand with mine and enjoy the hitch of her breath, giving away how she really feels even as her words say something entirely different. "All my focus has been on Rose since my divorce, as yours has been since Oliver died. You're doing a great job with the boys, and I know he would be proud of how you're handling everything considering. Anybody would be."

She smiles through her tears. "Thank you."

"You're welcome." Wrapping my fingers around her hand, I lift it up to my mouth and kiss the back, enjoying the sharp inhale of her breath as her eyes flutter closed. "I don't want to play games, sweetheart. You should know I haven't been with another woman since the time we spent together."

Her eyes fly open at that, her lips parting in surprise, and if I weren't so intent on making her understand where things stand between us, I would laugh.

"I convinced myself that taking care of Rose is why I haven't dated, but that's not entirely accurate. I walked out of that hospital room wishing things had gone differently between us and over the years, accepted I lost you because I couldn't see beyond the pent up anger when you came to my place."

"Zach." A tear slips down her cheek as her lower lip wobbles. "I can't—"

"Despite what you think, I don't want to push anything to happen between us. I merely want for us to at least become friends again and have the door left open for other, even more, amazing possibilities."

She stares at me, using her free hand to swipe at her tears, before tugging the other I'm holding away with an uncertain smile. "I'll think about it."

I let out the breath I hadn't realized I was holding. "A maybe is always better than a no."

"Yeah, well, you've always been pretty persuasive." She turns away, taking a deep breath and exhaling slowly before laughing at the kids, who are now all playing quietly in the sandbox. "Landon is covered."

And just like that, the subject is put to rest, for now. For her, because I've got nothing except time to wait. "You're going to have a hell of a time getting the sand out of his hair."

"He has a lot," she agrees with another snicker. "Just like Oliver..."

Her voice cracks as she trails off and this time when I cover her hand with mine in a show of comfort, she doesn't pull away.

We sit like that, watching our children play together as if they're best friends until the time to leave arrives, and when we part this time, Darcy hugs me first.

"I LIKE WYATT," ROSE DECLARES FROM THE back seat on the drive home, her expression happy and excited. "He's nice."

"I'm glad, sweetheart."

"He doesn't like the swings as much as I do, but that's okay. I told him it's because he's not big like me and the swing will be more fun when he gets bigger."

I laugh. "Rose, he may not enjoy them when he gets older, either. Not everyone likes the same things, remember?"

"He's my brother," she replies with wide eyes as she meets my gaze in the rearview mirror. "I will help him so he will like swinging with me."

Like her father and mother, this one. Tenacious as hell when she wants to be. I'm going to have my hands full when she's a teenager. "Sure, sweetheart. Maybe he will like swings one day if you show him how fun they can be."

"I will." She nods, determined, and quickly switch topics with an impish smile as I focus my attention back on the road. "I like his mommy, too. Do you like her, Daddy?"

"I do."

"She's nice. You need a nice friend." She pauses for a second and then observes, "I saw her crying. Did you make her cry, Daddy?"

The question makes me wince. "Not on purpose." When she continues to wait in silence for an explanation, I consider how to explain Darcy's distress without oversharing, or trying to clarify why Wyatt thought someone else was his father. Not something she'll understand so I keep it simple. "She's been sad because Landon's daddy died and she misses him."

"Oh." She frowns and a quick glimpse shows she's crossed her arms over her chest, now staring out the window. "That's sad."

"It is. However, I think they had a lot of fun at the park today because of you. Maybe we'll go again next weekend."

I hear rather than see the gleeful clap of her hands. "Yes! I want to go next weekend!"

Me, too. Any chance to see Darcy and be there for her in whatever way she'll let me.

"All right," is what I say out loud to Rose. "I'll call and ask her later."

She's quiet for the rest of the ride home, giving me plenty of time to go over the conversation with Darcy in my head and mull over what the hell will happen if she ignores what's between us and decides giving a relationship between us another shot is out of the question.

DARCY

I told Zachary I would think about what he said and for the last week, it's among one of the few things I can't get out of my head.

His revelations weren't surprising. The attraction between us is strong as ever, and I don't believe that will ever change.

But telling me he hasn't been with anyone else since the incredibly hot sex we had against the door? I hadn't known what to say to that and still don't know what to think about it.

Or the warmth and tenderness in his eyes when he basically offered himself on a platter, declaring he doesn't want to push, but he'll be there, hoping for more.

Mostly because he saw through my line about the way things are being better for us, that I don't want him in my life. He knows I'm protecting my heart...or what functions as my heart at this point, which is still heavily damaged from the grief of losing Oliver.

If I'm completely, one-hundred-percent honest with myself, I don't know how long I can hold out. Emotionally and physically, I want and perhaps even need what he's offering me. When he touches me, even innocently, I want to lean into the caress and beg for more.

And each time these thoughts enter my mind, the guilt creeps in because it hasn't even been a year since Oliver died.

Yeah, everything I read says everybody grieves differently, and there isn't a timeline for when a person may move on from the death of a loved one, yet...damn.

The wrongness has settled in my chest because the more I want it, the more I tell myself it's too soon. That I should focus on my sons and keep Zach at arms' length because nothing good will come of us getting involved with each other again.

How can it, after everything?

Mostly, I'm sick of going over and over it in my head. Of being unable to get rid of the feel of his arms around me or dismiss the kiss, he placed on the top of my head.

I keep shoving it aside, trying to think about other things and focus on what I can control in my life, yet he keeps invading my thoughts and my dreams.

For the first time since before Oliver's death, I woke up this morning with the desire to have sex, already aroused from the dream I couldn't remember much of even as my hand rested between my legs.

I tried to keep going and bring myself to climax while conjuring my lovemaking with Oliver in my mind, but it hadn't worked. Frustrated, and wanting the relaxation getting off would give me, I gave in and thought of Zach. Heard his voice in my mind as I touched myself, imagining him giving me instructions and talking dirty to me, and it wasn't long before my body shook from the pleasure I wrung from it.

Only after, I cried because that's when I realized the sound of Oliver's voice is no longer something I can bring to mind by simply thinking of him. I'm slowly losing pieces of him, and he's being replaced by Zach — my first love and the father of one of my sons — whether my heart is ready for it or not.

And the tricky part is not knowing what to do because the longer I can't give a definitive answer about what step we take next, leaving him with the hope something else may happen, the harder it will be for all of us if the final answer is the last thing he wants to hear.

❦

"You should go dancing," my mother says as we eat breakfast, my father already gone since early this morning to run some errands.

A sharp pain burst in my chest at that because she's suggesting I do something on my own that was mine and Oliver's thing.

"I'm good," I mumble after taking a drink of orange juice. "Not in the mood to dance."

"Darling." She gives me the 'I'm your mother, and I know what's best for you' look and smiles. "When your father and I came to visit you for the holidays, you would dance around the house and hum. You were happy, and I would love to see you happy again, even if only for the joy of dancing and the way it makes you feel."

"I don't want to dance with anyone else."

Irrational, yet true. I learned with Oliver and neither of us ever danced with anyone else.

My mother lifts a skeptical brow and laughs softly. "So you'll never dance again for the rest of your life? That would be a waste of all the time you spent learning, and I'm sure Oliver wouldn't want you to stop."

No, he wouldn't. The issue is bigger than that, however. "Mother..."

"Darcy."

I explain with a sigh. "I finally stopped crying every time I think about him. I don't want to break down while dancing or...or..."

She says what I can't. "You aren't replacing him, darling. Nothing you do will ever take his place in your heart or your life. Dancing...dating..." She smiles at my scowl, rising from her seat with plate and glass in hand. "Yes, I've seen the way you look at Zach and who can blame you? He is one gorgeous man."

"What? I'm hardly in the same room with him more than two minutes when he comes to visit."

"Oh, honey." She takes the dishes to the sink and sets them inside before walking toward me. "You've never believed this, but your emotions are all that beautiful face of yours and shine from your eyes. Even when you thought you were successfully lying to your father and me, we always knew you weren't telling the truth. And right now, darling, the only person believing any lies is you."

My mouth drops open.

She grins at having shocked me into silence and pats my shoulder before giving it an affectionate squeeze. "Go dancing. Even for an hour or so. I'll watch the boys."

She's trying to help.

I recognize this. However, even after all these years, sometimes it's difficult to refrain from telling her to back off. Then I'll think back to the dream that felt so real as well as recall all those years we wasted not speaking, and the feeling usually goes away because some things just aren't worth fighting about. Nor are they worth fracturing our relationship once again.

In truth, nothing is wrong with her suggestion and what will it hurt by going to the dancing studio? I don't have to dance, but I can watch. Or I'll find something else to do for that hour if going there isn't something I can handle in the end.

Either way, getting out for a little while on my own isn't a bad idea.

"Okay," I finally respond, smiling up at her as her hand slips off my shoulder. "I will. Thanks."

"My pleasure, darling. Have a good time."

As she walks away, I call out, "Oh, and Mother? Please don't put any ideas into Zach's head just because I'm not here to stop you."

Her only response to that as she walks out of the kitchen is laughter.

I LEAVE A LITTLE BEFORE ZACH IS SUPPOSED TO arrive for his visit with Wyatt.

I don't send him a message telling him I won't be there before driving toward the dance studio. I try not to talk to him unless it's about Wyatt — which I know he dislikes — and honestly, I'm glad my mother made her suggestion.

Mostly because I'm not ready to face him or make a decision, but also because of the what ifs?

All these years, after everything we've both been through, and now we'll be together? Perhaps I shouldn't question if we should become romantically involved considering the way Wyatt turned out to be his son. A part of me thinks I'm being silly; another wonders if I'm not skeptical enough.

More than half my adulthood had been based on the decision I made when I was a teenager. That's changed. We both have, yet my main worry is really about our history. It's the past, but it's never forgotten, and it will always be a part of our story.

So, now what? Do we get a second chance as adults who have grown into better versions of ourselves and share a child? Maybe. And there's no point in denying wanting him or that I'm attracted to him as he is to me; not when even my mother sees it.

On the other hand, I'm scared of any attempt at a relationship burning us both and jeopardizing our co-parenting of Wyatt. That's a major cause of my hesitation, and I know Zach understands, which is why he said he'd be patient.

Even so, I'm sick of feeling this way — desiring Zach and wanting everything that comes with that while still missing Oliver so much that my heart aches when thinking of him.

Sighing, I pull into the parking lot of the studio, park close to the doors, and sit there watching people head inside for a few minutes while trying to talk myself into getting out of the car and going in.

The decision is made for me when my instructor, Louis, spots me sitting in the car and jogs in my direction.

I open the door and step out before he reaches me, his smile warm and welcoming as always while his eyes are soft with compassion because he hasn't seen me in nearly a year now. Of course, he knows what happens; everyone does.

"What a pleasure to see you, Darcy!" He steps forward and embraces me briefly before retreating with a sheepish smile at the shock on my face. "Sorry, guess I should've asked first."

"Uh, no, it's all right." And it is. "A hug from

someone I consider a friend is more than welcome. How's Greta? Is she here?"

"She's great!" He leans in as if he doesn't want others to hear and whispers, "She's not here; she had an appointment. We haven't made an official announcement, but she's pregnant."

I cover my mouth with both hands, trying to smother my excited reaction as happiness for them both makes coming here today worth it. "Oh, my god. How wonderful for you both!"

"Thank you. She will be sad she missed you as we have wondered how you've been."

No need to apologize for not calling them back. I can tell he understands by the way he's looking at me and respond with the only thing that matters. "I've missed you both, too, and dancing, honestly. It was hard for me to come here today, though."

"Well, I am pleased you did. Come inside, and if nothing else, you will dance with me to show these new people how it is done."

He leads the way inside as I laugh and before long, we're doing exactly that as he instructs the class. At first, I can't get Oliver out of my head, but then I really get into the way I feel and turn this day into something I need just for me.

And when he needs to assist others, he asks if I'm willing to dance with someone else. Because I'm here and having fun, not wanting it to end yet, he hands me off to a lone male in the back of the room.

"You're a beautiful dancer," the man murmurs as the music begins, his hands holding me firmly as we get into position. His gaze is beautifully dark and reminds me of Oliver, but his voice is deeper; his hair lighter. "I am Vincent. And you are...?"

"Darcy."

He grins as we begin moving and I quickly realize there's a reason Louis paired me with this man — his dancing is exquisite.

His warm hand on the small of my back tugs me closer as he chuckles, bringing his mouth closer to my ear to say, "It's nice to meet you."

My heart beats faster the closer he gets, the tighter he holds me, as he reminds me more of Oliver with each passing moment. I close my eyes, trying to shut out those thoughts, and manage to croak out, "You, too."

Neither of us speaks during the rest of the dance together and the sound of my phone ringing right as the dance ends saves me from having to say anything except, "Excuse me," as I walk over to answer the call.

Only the elation from dancing hums is replaced with dread at the call from Zach, and after grabbing my things, I flee from the studio without saying goodbye to head straight to the hospital.

Darcy's mother answers the door at my fourth weekly visit with Wyatt, and I don't attempt to hide my confusion. "Ah, hello. Is Darcy here?"

"Nope, but I am," she replies with a cheery smile as she steps back. "Come on in. Wyatt's just finished lunch and is playing in his room."

"Thanks."

Walking past her, I wonder where Darcy is. This is the first time she hasn't been at home when I've come over.

Her mother answers my question before I can ask as she shuts the door. "Darcy's gone to a dancing class. She'll be back in an hour."

"Darcy dances?"

"Yes." Her smile is soft and sad. "One of her and Oliver's favorite things to do. They were quite good, and of course, now that he's gone, she doesn't have anyone to dance with. I am glad to see her going to class to solve that problem, at least."

Interesting. When we were kids, the only dancing Darcy ever managed was to sway back and forth while trying not to step on my feet. "I have to admit I would like to see her dance."

"Perhaps you will. I believe we have you to thank for her cheerfulness lately?"

I laugh at that and slip out of my jacket. "Can't say I've been experiencing anything except her usual attitude with me, albeit with a less bite now than before, so no, I don't believe I'm the person you should be thanking."

"If you say so." She holds out her hand to take my jacket with a light laugh. "Go on. I'll put this away in the closet for you. Gil is waiting for me to finish lunch for us now that the boys have eaten."

Handing it over, I say, "Thanks, Paula," and head to Wyatt's room.

Usually, his smile is happy when he sees I'm visiting, but today, he doesn't even look up from where he plays with his cars on their special mat on the carpeted floor.

"Hey, buddy." I greet him softly while taking a seat on the floor nearby. "What are you doing?"

"Nothing," he mumbles, still not looking at me and instantly making me worry.

Then, his sniffling and wiping at his face give away the fact he's crying.

"Why are you upset, buddy? Talk to me."

"Mommy left," he whispers, his green eyes wide and filled with tears as he finally looks up at me. "I don't want her to die like Daddy."

Stunned into silence at his words, I open my arms in hopes he'll let me hold him, and he does. He scrambles into my lap and clutches at my shirt while continuing to cry as I try to find the right words to reassure him.

Rose didn't really fear or understand death until she turned seven and hasn't had to deal with someone she knows passing away. It had been hard enough with her; I'm not sure how Darcy would handle this with our almost-five-year-old son.

But since she isn't here and he needs me to say something, I use the discussion I had with Rose after speaking with her pediatrician about what the best way to have this conversation was.

"You know, Buddy, as humans, we are living things, along with plants and animals such as dogs and cats. When you were born, you were small like Landon, and now look at you. And one day, you might be as big or bigger than I am."

He hasn't looked at me, but his crying has subsided as he asks, "I will?"

"Yep. That's what growing up is, and growing

up means getting older. Some of us live longer than others, but at the end of our life cycle, we end up not living anymore because that's what happens with living things."

"I want to live forever."

"So do I, buddy. That would be cool, wouldn't it?"

He sits up and rubs his eyes, nodding. "And I want mommy to live forever with me so she won't leave."

"Aw, buddy, she didn't leave you. She just went dancing because it makes her happy. Your mommy would never leave and not come back on purpose. She loves you."

His face crumbles as he whispers, "I miss Daddy."

Fuck, at this point, he's making me want to cry with how heartbroken he is. "I know you do. Your mommy misses him, too."

After a few moments, he asks, "Did you know my Daddy?"

"A little. Not as much as your mom, who I've known for a long time." When he nods at that and climbs off my lap, I stand up and attempt to divert his attention. "How about we get something to drink? I'm thirsty."

"Okay."

Crouching down, I turn my back on him and

look over my shoulder to grin at him. "You're not too old for a piggy back ride, are you?"

"No!" He climbs on with a giggle and wraps his hands around my neck as I grab his legs.

Then, I carry him through the hallway and down the steps, turning right to head toward the kitchen. Darcy's parents are sitting at the table eating, and they both look up at the same time as we enter.

"We came to get something to drink," Wyatt explains to them as I crouch so he can slide off my back, his bare feet smacking against the tile floor as he lets go of my neck.

He heads over to the table and takes a seat beside his grandfather while I walk to the cupboard to grab two cups.

My back is turned as Paula asks, "Why are your eyes red, Wyatt? Were you crying?"

"Yeah. I was sad, but not anymore."

She's eyeing me as I walk back to the table with some juice for the both of us, and when she looks at me with her nervous eyes, I smile to let her know whatever upset him has been taken care of.

At least, I hope so.

Gil stands up, plate and cup in hand as he steps away from the table and winks at Wyatt. "Can't think of anything less fun than being sad."

Wyatt grins. "No more sad!"

Gil returns his grin with a loud chuckle and walks over to the sink, setting his plate and glass inside with a pronounced clink. "Good, sport."

Then, as he pivots to return to the table, he suddenly clutches his chest and drops to his knees on the kitchen floor, staring at us with wide-eyed terror as Wyatt shouts, "Granpa!"

"I WAS SO SCARED I WAS GOING TO LOSE HIM." Darcy's on her second glass of red wine and it isn't even nine o'clock, but she deserves it after spending most of the afternoon in the hospital. "Not sure I could handle that."

Hell, seeing her father hit the floor terrified me. Not only because of the way he'd gone sheet white, but Darcy's already fragile with Oliver's death. Anything else might put her over the edge she's barely managing to stay away from.

Calling to tell her to meet us at the hospital had been one of the hardest moments of my life, her instant shock and grief at what might happen apparent even over the phone.

"I'm glad he's all right." I take a seat beside her on the couch and sigh, sitting down for the first time since her father hit the kitchen floor earlier today. "As long as he does as the doctor recommends, he'll be better in no time."

"Severe heartburn, enough to bring him to his knees." She shakes her head. "He's always loved his spicy food. I don't see him adjusting all that well to the new restrictions."

"Nor will your mother," I reply, laughing. "Should've heard her wondering how she was going to manage the changes to their diet after all these years."

"Oh, I bet their chef is gonna love that. Pretty sure she hired the current one for his daring and inventive culinary skills."

"Poor guy. Hopefully, she'll give him a good reference."

She snorts at that and downs the rest of the wine before pouring herself another glass. Then, she readjusts in her seat until she's facing me, one leg bent beneath her on the couch, and stares at me while biting her lip.

Figuring she must be working up the courage to ask or say something, I give her the opening to do whichever she chooses. "What?"

She takes a deep breath before asking quickly, "Will you do me a favor?"

My answer is swift, decisive, and unthinking because I will do anything for her as long as it isn't illegal. Well, even then it's negotiable depending on the level of illegal involved. "Of course."

"Good." She releases that huge breath and says in a completely serious tone, "Have sex with me. Tonight."

Wow.

Not anywhere close to something I thought she would say. And without thinking about anything else except how this is a bad idea after the day we've had, I shake my head.

Her eyes grow misty, and she drops her gaze to her wine glass as she asks in a shaky, watery voice, "You don't want me?"

"God, Darcy, you know damn well I want you. But, not like this, sweetheart. If you decide to sleep with me, you'll need to tell me when you're sober and not emotionally upset by something that's happened."

"I don't know if I can." She begins sobbing into her wine glass, her eyes now refusing to meet mine as she practically curls into herself. "It feels like such a betrayal to Oliver most of the time."

Well, this feeling of hers is new to me, although not unexpected. "What?"

"He overlooked everything." She looks at me then, tears spilling down her cheeks from eyes filled with misery. "I told him what happened with you and he wanted me to stay anyway. I came to you and went back and there he was, steady as always. No questions, nothing. And he let you sit at the hospital, even knowing what we'd done because he cared about me. He knew I would want to see you, that I would need that closure. He was a good man who loved me despite my faults and we built a good life together. I loved him."

"I know."

"You wouldn't even be here if he hadn't died. I honestly doubt I would've seen the truth because I was so happy."

Although I've gathered how she feels over the past few months, nothing like getting drunk to make her completely honest. Truth hurts, but I can accept Oliver's death made her entire world raw in a way it wouldn't have been otherwise, if ever.

Even though I don't think she's listening to anything coming out of my mouth, I say, "I know that, too."

"But when I'm like this?" She takes another sip of her wine. "It's easier to let go, to enjoy the way you make me feel instead of feeling guilty about it and like I'm wrong for wanting it."

"You're not wrong, sweetheart. You'll regret it, though, come morning if you feel this bad over merely wanting it. And I don't want to fuck things up by having sex with you when you're this vulnerable."

"Stop telling me how I'll feel." She glares at me as if my refusal to have sex with her right now is the worst fucking betrayal ever. "I've had a bit to drink, Zach. It doesn't make me incapable of knowing what I want. Why can't you just do what I want for once without overanalyzing it?"

"I'm trying to do the right thing, hard as that fucking is." Shoving a hand through my hair, I bring our faces as close as possible without kissing her so she can see how much I desire to give her what she's begging for as we stare into each other's eyes. "I want you when you're all mine and not feeling as if you're betraying Oliver."

"I want to be held," she wails, drawing back and gulping down the last of her wine before leaning to place it on the side table and glaring at me when she sits straight once more. "Ten months I've been alone now, after thirteen years with him. I've sat on this...this damn couch watching TV by myself, or sleeping in our bed and not being held by my husband all these months. No cuddling, kissing, or touching from another adult, day in and day out. And I...I hate it. It's awful and when I think of how I'll never do any of those things with him ever again, my chest a-aches—"

That's it.

Unable to stand the despair in her eyes, I haul her into my arms and embrace her as she straddles my lap with a soft gasp of surprise, intent on being another adult cuddling and comforting her. Her warm body melts into my hold. She hides her face against my chest and slips her arms around my neck.

"I want this," she whispers, lifting her head to press a soft, warm kiss against my throat with her wine sweetened breath, and turning the innocent embrace into something else entirely. "I need this."

My resistance slips as she repeats the action with a little more urgency. "Darcy..."

She rocks her lower body and giggles at my groan. "Don't deny me. I want you, Zach. I'm thinking about you and only you right now. Isn't that enough?"

With a hard swallow I grip her hips and admit, "It should be."

Her head rises a little further, her mouth pecking the corner of my lips before she whispers against them, "Then why aren't we doing what we both want?"

"Dammit." Leaving one hand on her hip, I slide the other up her back and into the hair at the nape of her neck, clutching a handful in my fist as she moves against me once more. "I would be a fool to turn you down when you're sitting on my lap practically begging for it, sweetheart."

"Good." She sucks in a sharp breath when I tilt

her head back and expose the silken skin of her neck as I return her kiss with my own. "You've never been a fool so don't start now."

"Not true," I say before nipping at her, enjoying the hiss through her slightly parted lips and the way her nails suddenly dig into my shoulders through the soft cotton fabric of my button down. "I've been a fool plenty. None worse than when I let you walk out of my house that day without fighting for you. And you chose Oliver because he was there for you when I wasn't."

Although she had gone still at the mention of his name, it didn't last long as she rocked her hips and whispered, "Make it up to me, Zach. Be there for me now and give me what I need."

If I were a better man, I would carry her to bed and tuck her in before wishing her a goodnight, leaving her tipsy and aroused because it is the right thing to do. She would be mad at me, but she would probably get over it and thank me in the morning.

But the way she's begging, so sweet and hungry with want for the touch and affection I can give her, is impossible to resist. Nor am I idiotic enough to pass up on what might be my one opportunity to establish what we'll have together if she says yes to a second chance.

"I can't stay too long," I remind her, the idea of satisfying our mutual lust only to leave her to sleep alone not sitting well with me, although it's unavoidable. "I have to get home to Rose."

"I know." She bites her lip before admitting, "I think that's a good thing right now."

I nod, getting it. Sex is different from sleeping together — more personal, an invasion of the space she shared with Oliver and isn't ready for.

And as I told her, time is something I've got plenty of. So, I give in, bringing her head forward again until my mouth can devour hers, my tongue taking advantage of her delighted gasp to slip inside and deepen the kiss.

And with that decision, the line between Darcy and me, as well as the past and the present, is irrevocably crossed.

My only hope is that come morning, I'm not the one having regrets about being unable to deny her.

Zach carries me to my room, forcing me to relinquish my hold on him as he drops me on the bed and pivots away to shut the bedroom door.

The lock clicks, sending my heart racing, especially when he stalks toward the bed like a man on a mission.

Even though I'm only able to make out his silhouette in the darkened room, I watch him instead of shedding my own clothing, unable to believe he actually gave into my unexpected request.

I had no plans to ask him the question before the words popped out of my mouth, almost on their own, and yes, it was the influence of the alcohol.

But I'm not drunk.

Just horny, lonely, and really wanting to see if

the sex between us as is good as my memories let me believe they are when I allow myself to think of them.

Plus, after the dance in the studio today and my body's reaction to Vincent's similarities to Oliver, I want something familiar. Something I can touch and hold and that is all mine, even for only tonight; even if it's wrong for us to do this in the end.

This might be, but tonight...after the day we've both had, I don't care. And tomorrow morning, I probably will; Zach wasn't wrong about that.

My thoughts are interrupted by the bed dipping beneath his weight, and within a breath he covers me with his fully dressed form, leaving me unable to escape as my body responds with urgent arousal to his closeness.

He presses his face into the side of my neck, nipping at the skin with his teeth before soothing the sting with a light lick of his tongue.

One of his hands spears my hair as he brings his mouth to mine without preamble, my lips parting under pressure from his. He growls when my tongue touches his and I wrap my arms around his neck while lifting my body up to rub against his.

We go from full clothed to completely naked with our lips only parting once during the whole thing when we both remove our shirts simultaneously. His skin feels hot and amazing against mine and in this the experience with him is all new.

Against that door, we were both dressed and this is nothing like when we were teenagers when he was less broad and muscly. I love the way his body is unfamiliar and different even though he's not in the ways that count.

"God, you have a gorgeous body," he says as he comes up for air, his words rough and husky as he grips both my hips and grinds his arousal against me.

I roll my hips, trying to entice him to proceed. When his clutch tightens to prevent our bodies from connecting, I laugh and respond to what he's said. "There's no way you can see me in here."

"I don't need to. You're fucking stunning, Darcy, and always have been." One warm hand leaves my hip and slides up the side of my body before closing over the soft flesh of my breast — definitely bigger than the last time he touched it — and he smiles against my mouth while stroking the nipple with the pad of his thumb. "Even more so with the addition of these stunning curves. I could play with your body for hours."

"We don't have hours," I remind him with another lift of my hips, my moan mingling with his as he kisses me once more while pinching my nipple into a stiff peak in response.

He chuckles into my mouth as my arms tighten around his neck. "Don't rush me."

Rushing is exactly what I want. I'm desperate for the connection of having him inside me, stroking in and out while our mouths mesh in a raw and purely physical way. I want hot and fast sex, not a slow love making session. Not tonight.

Turning my head to the side, away from his mouth so he can't silence me, I tell him, "Go faster."

Then I unclasp my hands and slide one down his sleek back until I reach his hip, then go around to slip it between our bodies. My fingers wrap around his cock, and he groans as I stroke him up and down in the firm hold of my fist.

"You said you would give me what I need, Zach." I pause on the downstroke, thoroughly enjoying the way he's frozen in my grasp, his mouth having moved to lick and suck at the nipple he played with. I know desperation laces my words now and I don't care because my whole body is on fire. "And what I need is you inside me, right now."

He doesn't move to give me what I want, lifting his head and using his free hand to grab my chin before turning my face until our mouths meet. Then, he grins, nips at my lower lip, and thrusts into my hand. "When did you get so demanding?"

I give him another squeeze, not answering, and relish the tensing of his body in my hold.

"Fuck, Darcy." Both his hands land on the bed, one of each side of me, as he lifts his body away from mine a little and growls, "What has gotten into you?"

I release my hold on his dick with a snicker. "Not you, at this rate."

Rumbling laughter, but no comeback. He readjusts, then slips a hand down between my thighs and pushes two fingers inside me. My gasp is lost in his kiss as he covers my mouth and curls his fingers to stimulate my g-spot while teasing my clit with his thumb. Over and over until I would beg for release if his mouth weren't preventing me from doing so.

He moves again, thrusting his cock inside me seconds after his strokes coax an intense and overwhelming orgasm, and his weight comes back down on me like an anchor meant to keep me from floating away.

My hands are seized, held above my head as he fucks me hard and fast as if he knows anything gentler is out of the question. He's giving me exactly what I want and need, only to suddenly withdraw before rolling away from me and sitting on the edge of the bed.

"Zach?" I sit up and move to his left side, finding his bare thigh and resting my hand on it. "Is something wrong?"

"I need to go."

That's a yes. "Now you're in a rush to leave?" I move my hand to his cock, still hard and ready to go, but before I can grab him, he stands up.

Then he drops a kiss on the top of my head and walks away without replying, the swoosh of him picking up his clothes the only sound in the now pitch black room.

I'm lost, tears pooling in my eyes and gliding down my cheeks as the loneliness that went away for a short time while in his arms returns with a vengeance. Aware this is my fault even if I don't know exactly how, I listen to him finish dressing in silence, and when he opens the door, I turn my head into my shoulder so he can't see me crying.

I hear him say, "We'll talk tomorrow," before shutting the door behind him with a soft click as he leaves me all alone, just as I told him was best earlier.

Only now the last thing I want is to be alone, and I curl into a ball, sobbing my eyes out until they no longer stay open and I drift into my first restless sleep since Zach's re-entrance into my life.

THE NEXT AFTERNOON, I'M SORE, AND MY

mother won't quit frowning at me as we sit in the living room watching cartoons with the boys.

Mostly because I look like shit with the bags under my bloodshot eyes; basically, my appearance for over half a year after Oliver died when I couldn't stop crying.

She's already offered to watch the boys three times today so I can nap, but that's the last thing I want to do. Zach's scent is all over my bed now and the desire to wrap the blankets around me to surround myself is as strong as the one to throw the stuff in the washer to get rid of it.

And he hasn't messaged me or called. So many hours left in the day, yet it does say something because he's usually sent me quite a few messages before breakfast is even over.

I could message him; ask him the one thing I want to know more than anything.

Does he regret it? Is that why he stopped before finishing and left me without much more than a polite goodbye between us? He was hesitant and yeah he could've completely turned me down, but I pushed him hard to give me what I wanted without caring about his reasonable objection.

Ugh.

Holding Landon close — he's sound asleep in my arms — I turn the TV off and rise from the chair, smiling at Wyatt when he glances over his shoulder to see why his show isn't playing.

"Come on," I tell him while turning toward the doorway that leads to the hallway. "Lunch time."

"Great idea," my mother chimes in. "I'm starving."

Wyatt runs past my me and my mother's hand on my shoulder halts my progress toward the kitchen.

"Go lay Landon in his bed, darling, and get a little rest. I'll look after him."

"Mother—"

"Just go." She cuts in over my weak protest in a stern voice I haven't hear from her since I was a teenager. "I don't know what went on last night, but something did, and you don't have to fill me in if you don't want to. But you will go get some rest because you need it, for heaven's sake."

I don't have the energy to argue, suddenly more tired than I have been in ages.

After putting Landon in his room, I can't bear the thought of going back to my own. Instead, I walk to the guest room and shut myself inside, crawling in the freshly made up bed with sheets that don't smell like anything except laundry soap, and am asleep not long after I slip beneath the thick comforter.

THE GUEST ROOM HAS DARKENED considerably when I finally wake up from my nap, and I toss the comforter aside, eyes widening at the time flashing on the clock: five-thirty!

I slide out of bed and head downstairs, only to pause in the doorway and rub my eyes, but the sight before me doesn't change.

What the hell?

Zach sits in the living with Rose and the boys. Landon cuddles in Zach's lap as if he's been there since the day he was born, while Wyatt and Rose sit next to each other a few feet from the TV, giggling at the antics of the characters from some cartoon I don't recognize.

There's total silence throughout the rest of the house otherwise, so where are my parents and why didn't they wake me before leaving?

When I step inside the room, Landon sees me first and starts squirming, reaching his arms out to me as he babbles.

Of course, Zach's attention is on me now too, and he rises from the chair with Landon in his arms to walk over to me.

Wyatt and Rose glance my way, both going back to watching TV after waving at me with big, happy smiles.

Zach's expression is pretty neutral as he stops and hands Landon over, his gaze flicking down the length of me before returning to my face.

Landon's arms wrap around my neck as he snuggles into my embrace and when Zach doesn't say anything, I ask, "Where are my parents?"

"They went out to dinner." He tilts his head in the direction of Rose and Wyatt. "She asked me if we could come over so they could play. I called you to ask, and your mother answered. She said you were resting, and they had plans, but she didn't want to wake you. So if I didn't mind...?"

Sounds like something my mother would do. She probably found it funny because I definitely would've preferred she woke me up instead of inviting him over without asking first. "Ah. Well, thank you. How long have you been here?"

"Just over an hour." He ruffles Landon's hair. "We've had a good time, haven't we buddy?"

Landon giggles, peeking out at Zach before hiding his face against my throat like usual, and Zach shakes his head before flicking his gaze to mine.

"I ordered a pizza. Should be here soon," he says with a quick glance over at the kids. "They were hungry, and that was what they chose when asked. Hope that's all right."

"I slept way longer than intended. My opinion

doesn't really matter considering it's already ordered, does it?" He stares at me in silence, unsmiling, and I really can't handle the aloof way he's being anymore. "I'm going to feed Landon."

Pivoting, I walk away, and he doesn't say anything or stop me, bringing back all the unpleasant emotions from last night.

And although it's difficult to hold back my tears, I do. There's always time to let them out later when he's not around to witness how upset I am at the way he's acting.

So I focus on feeding Landon and then join them to eat when the pizza arrives, attempting to hold it together until we're all finished, and he can head home with Rose.

Only it doesn't happen that way.

Landon falls asleep in my lap during the meal, and after I return from placing him in his crib, Rose and Wyatt run off to play in his bedroom while Zach walks over to the sink.

"Oh, please just leave those," I say as he goes to turn on the water. "I'll get them later."

He pauses, hand hovering above the knob, and sighs. Then he turns around, leans against the counter, and slips his hands into the pockets of his jeans.

Despite the fact I don't really want to talk to him, he's here and watching me as if he's waiting for me to say something, so I decide to get it over with.

Taking a deep breath, I cross my arms over my chest and ask the one thing that's bothering me the most.

"What did I do wrong?"

His laughter is unexpected and the tears I've been holding back break free.

I'm not sure what the hell she's talking about.

Figuring she's joking, I laugh at her question, but sober instantly when her face falls, and she begins sobbing.

"Darcy?" I stride over when she cries harder and stop in front of her, helpless in my confusion as to why she's upset. "Why are crying? 'What did you do wrong?' What are you talking about?"

Her eyes narrow as she steps back and shakes her head, taking a deep breath as the tears stop as quickly as they arrived. "You know what? I'm not in the mood for this. You need to go."

Guess she's going to make me work for the reason behind her annoyed disposition tonight. "In the mood for what?"

"For this!" She waves her hands wildly in my direction even though her voice remains soft and calm in spite of her obvious agitation. "This back and forth guessing game or whatever this is."

"Then we're on the same page, sweetheart because I have zero idea what the hell is going on or why you're pissed right now."

"Me?" She lifts her hands, palms up, while her mouth hangs open a bit until she snaps it shut and glares at me. "You're the one who got up and walked out last night without an explanation."

Now I'm confused. That's what her attitude has been about since she saw me sitting in the living room earlier?

Trying to clarify, I rub my forehead, looking down as I ask, "What does my leaving — as I said I needed to — have to do with you believing you've done something wrong?"

"Zach." She says my name as if I've just asked a stupid question, then continues on to point out exactly why she believes it is one. "We were in the middle of having sex and you literally stopped, got up and dressed, and left with nothing more than a 'we'll talk tomorrow' before you walked out."

"Huh." Missing something obvious here, I lift my head and discover her frowning at me. "I'm not understanding the problem here. I give you exactly what you want and then head home, and you take it personally?"

"Oh, my god." She covers her face with both

her hands and releases a growl of frustration. "Just forget it."

"No, baby, we won't forget it." Stepping closer, she doesn't see me coming with her face covered, and her squeak of surprise as I press her against the doorframe is charming. She refuses to look at me as I bend to kiss her neck, then ask, "Do you regret last night? Is that what this is about?"

She scoffs. "No. I wasn't drunk. I knew what we were doing." I wait for her to elaborate on what this is about and she finally gives in with a sigh. "You didn't....you didn't even finish, all right? You got me off, and then you got *off* me and left."

If I didn't think she'd punch me for laughing right now, I would, so I settle for a grin. One she glares at me for as she finally looks up at me when I ask, "That's it?"

"No." She bites her lip as it begins to tremble. "The way it ended made me feel awful. Yes, like I had done something wrong. I wanted you to go faster, and you did, then suddenly it was over and no cuddling or anything. It was like you couldn't even get out of the room fast enough."

Damn. "I'm sorry you saw it that way, sweetheart. Leaving you was the last thing I wanted to do."

"Could've fooled me. And then earlier, you didn't even smile when you saw me."

Definitely not smiling now as her words wobble with hurt, the last thing I thought she would be feeling after last night, and I try to explain. "Darcy, last night we weren't using anything, and perhaps you haven't noticed this, but I have this amazing ability to get you pregnant despite my attempts not to."

Her entire face flushes because she hadn't considered that at all. "Really? You couldn't ask me if I had condoms?"

"Do you?"

She glances away, biting her lip even as her lips quirk up in repressed laughter. "No, but you could've at least asked."

"Yeah, sweetheart, you gave me plenty of chances to slow down and ask questions last night." Turning her face to mine, I press my mouth against hers and run my tongue along her lips until she opens them with a sigh, her whole body losing the tension I've no doubt she's carried around since last night. I draw back then and murmur, "As for not letting you use that beautiful hand of yours on me last night, there's not a chance in hell I would've done the right thing if I hadn't left immediately."

She sniffles, lifting her hands to rest on my shoulders with a sheepish smile, desire shining in her eyes. "I guess I forgive you then."

"Yeah?" I grab her hand and drag it between

our bodies, guiding her to the results of our close proximity while whispering in her ear, "Enough for a repeat of last night after the kids are in bed for the night, except with a better ending?"

"Zach..."

"Hm?"

I wait for her denial of my request; I'm prepared for it. Her hand rests where I placed it, her gaze searching mine as if she's trying to gather the strength to turn me down amidst her internal struggle between desire and grief.

But she surprises me as only she can do when she lifts a brow, flexes her hand, and asks with a light laugh, "Did you bring something to ensure it has a better ending?"

"Yes."

"You planned this."

"I did."

She glances toward the stairway as the kids' laughter filters downstairs and then back at me with uncertainty. "You want to spend the night...?"

"I didn't plan on it, but now, absolutely. Rose will love the idea of a sleepover, and after I've fucked you unconscious, I'll move to the couch."

"Zach!" She can't even get my name out without laughing, bring her hand up to cover her mouth and making me groan by squeezing my cock to remind me of where the other is. "Watch your language!"

"They can't hear me." Stepping back, I snatch that hand in mine before she entices me to take things further than we should and glance around the kitchen. "Where's the laundry room?"

"Um, over there." She nods toward at the door on the opposite side of the kitchen. "Why?"

"Because Landon is sleeping, the other two are playing, and we're going to take advantage of the moment while it lasts."

"What?"

Her voices rises in alarm as I lead her across the room. She tugs on her hand but doesn't really endeavor to get away, and once we're in the laundry area, I back her against the wall next to the door.

"See?" I tell her while unbuttoning her jeans, tipping my head to demonstrate my view into the kitchen. "I can see or hear them if they head down the steps or scream. Don't worry."

"Zach, we can't have sex right now," she objects while shoving her hands through my hair, her face flush with desire and embarrassment. "Let's wait until they're asleep."

"No sex." I tug her jeans and panties down far enough to slip my hands into the tight space between her legs, keeping her pressed against the wall and unable to escape with my body as I whisper into her ear, "Just you and this gorgeous body of yours coming while riding my hand."

And she does, beautifully, clinging to me even as she falls apart in my arms.

Being alone with her tonight can't come soon enough.

LONG AFTER THE KIDS ARE ASLEEP, DARCY rests her left hand on my chest and hooks a leg over mine with a contented sigh.

I skim my fingers down the soft skin of her bare back and bury my nose in her hair. She cuddles closer, breathing lighter and steadier as the second's pass, which cuts into any opportunity to talk if she falls asleep.

And we need to because I don't want to push her into something she isn't ready for, even if she's naked in my arms two nights in a row.

"Darcy."

"Mm?"

"Me being here tonight...is it too much for you?"

"No." She readjusts her position, not even bothering to lift her head while answering. "I thought it would be, but I'm glad you're here."

I wait for her to continue and she doesn't let me

down because, despite all these years, the way she shares her feelings hasn't changed in the slightest.

"Yesterday, on the way to the dance studio, I thought about everything between us, wondering if we should be together; if we should risk messing things up now that we've got Wyatt to think about."

"I know."

She coughs and sits up, running a hand through her hair before resting it on my stomach. "Do you remember me mentioning a dream that day at the hospital?"

The one thing I remember from the hospital is wishing things were different and she was going home with me. Everything else is a blur. "Sorry, I don't. My mind was on other things."

"It's okay. But, you're the only person I mentioned it to. Not even Oliver knew about it."

"Why?"

"Because it wasn't a mere dream. I hit my head, and while you two were waiting for me to wake up, I was..." She shakes her head. "You're going to think I'm crazy."

"As if I don't already?"

"Shut up." She joins me in laughing for a moment before her expression turns serious. "Are you sure you want to know?"

"If you remember a dream after this long when

I can't remember what I ate for dinner every day last week, then it must be important."

"You were in it."

If she didn't already have my full attention, that would certainly get it. "Oh?"

"Yep. But the life I woke up in, it was different. You and I had two kids — a boy and a girl — and were divorced. I was...I was remarried, to Oliver, with a baby on the way."

Can't say this out loud, but sounds more like a nightmare than a dream to me. "It wasn't real."

"That's the thing. I woke up in the hospital with that in my head. It was what our lives might have been. Even if it was just a dream, it felt so damn real." After she relays the entire thing to me, I have no idea what to say, and she waves a hand in the air. "Why do you think this whole situation has bothered me? I owned my choices when I woke up and yet, here we are, nearly six years later, right back in each other's lives. What was the point?"

"Darcy." I sit up, pull her into my arms, and lie back down with her on top of me. "We're here because we fucked up and share a son who needs his parents. There isn't a point or lesson or anything here for either of us, except to make sure we use a fucking condom if we aren't actively trying to have a child."

Her giggle is perfect — relief and amusement

rolled into one — as she relaxes into my embrace. "You believe it's that simple?"

"I've spent the last few years understanding everything isn't always the way we want it, but it doesn't mean our lives aren't exactly what we need."

"And this?"

"Whatever you want it to be, sweetheart. You know what I want, but even that's not what happens, I'm not going anywhere. I'll say those words as often as you fucking need me to."

"Okay."

"The only thing I don't want is for you to let fear of the unknown decide for you because nobody on this whole damn planet had any idea what will happen tomorrow."

"I do."

"Really?" She laughs when I roll her onto her back and start kissing her neck. "Feel free to share."

She doesn't, too distracted by my renewed attention on her body, and eventually she dozes off after requesting I don't move to the couch as planned.

And with no desire to deny her, falling asleep with her in my arms becomes a perfect ending to the day.

Zach spending the night and waking up in the same bed with me had been a new experience for us. So had breakfast with the kids before he left with Rose to go back home.

Before then, he pulled me somewhere private and kissed me goodbye long enough to make me wish we could go back to bed.

Of course, we couldn't. And now, almost a week later, I still can't believe I let him stay the night nor that I asked him to remain in bed with me with the risk of Wyatt finding his way into my room during the evening.

Not that he did, nor had the kids noticed.

My parents, however, were an entirely different story, and my mother's been waiting for me to tell her about it since after he left that morning.

The problem is, I don't know what to say. I've got zero ideas about what the hell I'm doing, and I can only be extremely glad for the infinite patience Zach has developed as an adult.

He's letting me lead the way forward, and part of me wishes he wouldn't. He has no issue with taking me into the laundry room while the kids are wide awake upstairs and pinning me against the wall while getting me off with his hand or shoving a few condoms to protect me into his pocket just in case the opportunity to have sex with me again arises.

I know why he can't do that when it comes to the relationship part of us. He can't make me be with him, or choose him, or let him into my life unless that's where I want him to be.

And I do. I really do. There's no point in pretending otherwise, not to myself, or my parents, or him. How can I when he obviously cares for our son and me enough to wait?

That's the crux of the problem; moving forward is what I'm struggling with the most. Trusting we're different people who have grown up and can have a successful relationship not marred by the past we share. And we're parents, which brings a whole other dynamic to what we will have together.

Plus, the sex was fantastic — way better than ever before — and worth keeping in mind.

One good thing is, the guilt over me feeling this way less than a year after Oliver died has diminished. He would want me to be happy — there were so many times he made clear how my well-being was what mattered to him most, more than anything else in his life.

Zach called it when I told him about that dream, pointing out how I fear the unknown. Yes, I do, based on what's occurred and knowing nothing is preventing my happiness from being ripped away from me at any moment in time with no warning.

And instead of embracing what he's offering, I'm doing the opposite because the pain of losing the man I spent thirteen years broke my fucking heart to the point I'm not sure I want it to feel that way ever again.

So, the issue is me, and the only question is, how the hell do I get over it before it costs me a relationship with the father of my child and the man who's never stopped loving me?

"Are you going dancing today?" My mother peeks at her watch and smiles at me as we sit in the living room watching some educational kids show with the boys. "You've got about thirty minutes to get there if you are."

"I wasn't planning on it."

"Why not?"

"Just hadn't planned on it. Last week was fun…"

I trail off, unsure if I want to go into details, but of course, she won't let me off the hook.

"But?"

"Yes, I love dancing. And yes, it was nice, and I enjoyed it. At first, it became about me and how much I love dancing." I smile at her sadly. "But then Louis paired me with this man who moved beautifully and reminded me of Oliver."

"And this man is why you won't go today?"

"Not the only reason. A part of it. Just hard to separate Oliver from dancing when we learned together."

She reaches over and covers my hand. "I suspect doing so will become easier the more you go and enjoy yourself. There are many activities your father and I like together, but we are able to enjoy them without each other as well. And as for this man in your class…" She winks at me and glances at Wyatt. "I wouldn't worry about him because it's obvious where your heart is. All you have to do is accept the truth in your head instead of fighting it."

"I know."

"Do you?" Removing her hand from mine, she

reaches out to Landon, who goes to her with a happy smile as I nod. "Then what are you waiting for, darling?"

"You don't think it's too soon?"

"No. I don't believe you should follow an arbitrary timeline on anything. If you want Zachary in your life in more than just his role as Wyatt's father, then that's what you should do."

I bite my lip, trying to keep my emotions in check, but tears find their way into my eyes anyway between mainly her permission to feel the way I do about Zach and my admission. "I'm scared of us not working out...and of losing him, too."

Her eyes are sympathetic even as her words are logical and a tad critical. "There is no certainty things between you two will work out, just as there isn't a guarantee it won't. As for losing him, we all fear people we love passing away. Almost four decades with your father and last week, I watched him drop to the floor. Scared me, darling, but it wasn't the first time nor will it be the last. And being afraid of Zachary dying isn't a rational reason to turn him away."

She makes it seem so simple. I wonder if Zach sees it that way if he also believes there's no point in wasting time, since I know he doesn't want me being afraid of something bad happening.

"You've grown so much," my mother continues

when I don't say anything. "Don't overthink it. Live your life, darling, and be happy. Whatever that involves. You and these boys deserve it."

I can't disagree there. Wyatt and Landon deserve every bit of happiness I can give them.

And perhaps I am putting too much thought into this.

That's why later on, after making sure my mother will watch the boys once they are in bed, I send Zach a message asking him if I can come over to talk once Rose is in bed and am out the door the moment he answers yes.

ZACH GREETS ME WITH A HUG AND A SWEET, short kiss after opening the door, then lets me inside and slips his hand into his pockets while leading us into the living room.

Sitting on the couch, he tugs me down beside him, puts an arm around my shoulder, and draws me into the comfort of his embrace before simply saying, "I'm listening."

Resting my arm around his waist, I close my eyes and tease him, "You don't want to guess the reason I'm here?"

He answers with a smile, his tone suggestive. "If teasing is what you came over for, sweetheart,

I'm happy to oblige after you tell me what you wanted to talk about."

Nervous as hell, I take a deep breath and keep my eyes shut tight while diving right in. "I came over to talk about us."

"Mm-hm." His hand strokes my bare arm, his head tilting to rest against mine. "Go on."

I'm glad he isn't looking at me in the eyes. I think it'll be easier to get it all out this way.

"My fear goes deeper than things going wrong between us. I lost Oliver, and it was devastating." My voice quavers as it always does when I think about him and I inhale slowly before letting it out just as slow before continuing on. "I realize I don't and can't control everything, but it doesn't stop the worry. That's what holds me back the most — the terrifying possibility of losing you, too."

He sucks in a breath, his hand on my arm pausing in its caress. "Darcy—"

"Wait. Let me finish, please." He remains silent instead of replying, and I sniffle, snuggling further into his warmth. "Against so many odds, we're in each other's lives again, and you were right that day in the park. I never thought I would see you again then, and after that day in the hospital, the same thing. I had this whole life with Oliver, and I thought that was it. And so did you."

"That is true."

"So, here we are, and nothing is like I thought it would be. And despite me telling myself how being with you is not a good idea, my heart won't listen. Because it's you; after all this time, you're the one my heart wants. And I'm scared." I'm too upset now despite my attempts to control my emotions, and the tears start falling. "You want me, and I want to give us a chance, and I'm just s—so afraid—"

"Baby." He pulls me onto his lap, kissing the top of my head when I bury it in his chest and wraps his arms around me tight. "I wish I could say the words you need to hear, but the only promise I can make is this one: as long as I have some say over what's going on, you won't lose me. That's a fucking guarantee."

I cry harder at that. Not because I don't believe him, but because hearing him say it brings such unexpected relief to my mind and the ache in my chest. While the fear is still there and may take some time to get past, the feeling of being suffocated under the weight of my distress dissipates a bit.

And when I can finally say something without stumbling over the emotional words, it's to make sure he understands what this means. "I need you to promise we can go slow, for all our sakes. Not forever, but…"

He picks up where I trail off with ease. "Enough for the progression to feel natural instead of out of nowhere?".

"Yes."

"Of course." He runs one hand down to my waist and begins playing with the edge of my shirt. "We'll go at whatever pace makes you comfortable." He pauses and then laughs softly into my hair. "I have one final question before we go celebrate this decision."

My stomach tightens at the implications of his statement even as the anxiety rears its head once more even though I don't know what he's going to ask. "What is it?"

He pauses and then whispers in my ear, "Are we done having children?" When I jerk in his hold, he releases me, and I lift my head to discover him grinning at me with a curious expression. "What?"

"Nothing. It's a legitimate question."

"And?"

"I haven't thought about it. Oliver and I...um, we didn't try for Landon, but we weren't avoiding it either. Why?"

He slides a hand behind my neck, pulls me in for a long, passionate kiss, and then murmurs against my lips, "Because I would love to have another child or two with you when we're ready for it."

There are a dozen things I could say to that, but in such a happy moment between us, I pick the one closest to the hope in my heart where everything works out between us.

"I would like that, too. One day."

In response, he stands up and carries me toward his bedroom to make good on his promise of a celebration and loving me forever.

EPILOGUE
DARCY

18 months later...

"Sweetheart, have you seen my damn ties?"

"No," I call out to Zach through the closed door as my mother presses her lips together to keep from laughing. "I assume they're in one of these *damn* boxes littering the house because they haven't been put away yet."

"They were in their own box and marked to go to our bedroom," he retorts. "They aren't there."

"Your ties require their own box?" My mother loses her battle, snickering softly at the absurdity like I want to, but remains silent while buttoning up the back of my dress. "Perhaps next time you'll pack them with something important, such as your suits."

"Next time?" He growls at me and makes a

promise we both know he'll keep. "Just wait until I find those ties."

"Good luck!"

After he walks off, my mother rolls her eyes and stands up, her hands grabbing the veil off the nearby chair to place it on my head. "I hope you are prepared for decades of those sorts of everyday conversations."

"I am." I don't need to tell her anything beyond that; we're both aware he's spent all his free time with us until two weeks ago when we moved into a house we bought together. When she rests her hands on my shoulders after placing my veil, I smile at her. "Thank you, Mom, for everything. I'm going to miss you and dad when you leave tomorrow."

She blinks rapidly, scolding me even though her tone is pleased. "Don't mess up my makeup, darling. Your father and I will be a phone call away if you need us."

"I know."

"Not that you will. Zachary has shown he's the kind of man who makes sure you have everything you need."

There's a knock at the door before I can agree with her about that, and when we both turn to see who's walking in, my two little partners in crime grin at us while shutting the door.

"Mom! We're hiding from Landon!" Wyatt's

breathing hard, dressed in his little suit for the wedding, and holding Rose's hand. "He won't leave us alone!"

Nothing to do except laugh because this is an ongoing problem. "You're his big brother, and he loves you, Wyatt. He doesn't understand when you don't want to play or why; he just wants to spend time with you."

I turn my gaze to Rose, who hasn't said anything and is staring at me. "Do you like your dress?"

"Yes, it's so pretty!" She releases Wyatt's hand and twirls, giggling as the skirt of her maroon dress fluffs out as she turns. "I'm going to wear it to school on Monday!"

"All your friends will be jealous, I'm sure," my mother chimes while holding her hand out to them both and directing her comment at Wyatt. "Let's go take our seats and give your mother a few minutes to herself."

Wyatt takes her hand, but Rose shakes her head and looks at me again. "I want to stay."

When I nod it's okay, figuring Rose intends to talk to me alone — she's been doing that a bit more lately when they're here, much to Zach's chagrin — my mother leads Wyatt out the door and leaves us alone in the room.

I've enjoyed getting to know her over the last

year and a half; she's a sweet girl. "What's on your mind, honey?"

"I have a question and my dad already told me I had to ask you for an answer."

"Sure! What is it?" Her expression conveys her uncertainty, so I take a seat and hold out my hand toward her. "You can always ask or tell me anything."

She grabs it and steps close until she can whisper, "Well, you're marrying my daddy today, and I wondered if...if that means you'll be my mom."

Aware of how her mother hasn't been involved with her since the divorce, I answer softly, "If you want me to be your mom, honey, then yes. I would love that."

Her grin is beautiful and delighted. She lets go of my hand and jumps into my arms, wrapping her arms around my neck and pressing a kiss to my cheek.

She allows me to reciprocate for a moment before pulling away and grabbing my hand again to tug on it. "Okay. Daddy's waiting, and I told him I would bring you down with me."

Laughing, I grab my skirt with my free hand and take a final glance in the mirror before smiling at her. "I'm ready. Lead the way!"

She does, all the way to the backyard where our

friends and family are waiting for the wedding to begin, before running off to sit at the front near Zach's parents.

Then, the music begins as my father offers his arm and walks me down the aisle.

A far cry from my first courthouse wedding with Oliver, but things were different, and I'm glad my parents get to be here this time around.

Plus, seeing Zach watching me from the archway altar sans tie with love shining from his eyes makes me grateful for everything in this moment, as I have tried to be every day since going to his house and sharing my fears with him.

Today is the result of hard work on both our parts — him keeping his promise about being there no matter what while I let him in and didn't let fear ruin us having a future together.

And now we're going to become a family.

My father kisses my cheek, taking a seat beside my mother as I step up next to Zach and face him. He takes my hands in his, locking our gazes and grinning as the ceremony begins, marrying us to each other on the exact day we met a lifetime ago as teenagers.

He kisses me, softly and sweetly, when we're pronounced husband and wife. Everyone's amused when I wrap my arms around him as he goes to pull back, extending the kiss, until we finally separate with our own laughter.

With the informality of our wedding meaning our reception is right outside with the event, the kids run up to Zach and me after, hand-in-hand, and surround us with hugs.

Zach leans over where they cling to us for another kiss, which I accept with a happy giggle, and is made better by his murmured, "I love you," once he ends it.

"I love you, too," I whisper back, appreciating the moment as he gazes at me with such affection before asking, "Did you find the ties?"

The naughty glint I've seen in his eye more and more lately returns with an equally wicked grin on his lips as he assures me, "I'll show you later."

Another promise made that will make for an enjoyable evening and a beautiful beginning to the rest of our life together.

It's everything I want and need, and when he takes my hand to pull me into our first dance together as a married couple, the only thing I'm worried about is if he's going to step on my feet.

He doesn't.

THE END!

**I hope you've enjoyed Zach and Darcy's story!

Thanks for reading and leaving a review is much appreciated!**

Join my reader's list by visiting my website (authorviolethaze.com) to stay up-to-date on new releases, giveaways, events & more. Plus, receive a FREE copy of **Forever His**!

ABOUT THE AUTHOR

Violet Haze is a big fan of writing and reading romance. The autistic mother of one, she currently spends her days writing, reading, procrastinating, playing violin and learning guitar, & listening to her son play video games she doesn't understand.

For information on other books you can read, including links to ALL the vendors, visit her website:
www.authorviolethaze.com!

Want to contact Violet?
Email her at: violet@authorviolethaze.com
Locate her by searching "Violet Haze" on Instagram, Facebook, and Twitter!

I hug her, feeling and hearing her surprised intake of breath, but her astonishment doesn't last long as she embraces me right back. I don't know why I did it, but her sudden sniffle makes me wanna cry, and when I pull back we give each other shaky smiles. Then, she squares her shoulders, turns around once more after a small wave of goodbye at Benedict and me, and walks away.

"I think," Benedict whispers into my ear as he slips his arm around my shoulders. "After that, we need to dance. Shall we?"

"Yes, please. And then I'd like a drink or two."

And we do.

Benedict leads me onto the dance floor, and after a few faster dances, followed by a slow one, we head back to the bar to have a few drinks.

Sometime during the night, I wonder if I'll ever get to the level of acceptance Rissa seems to have managed. And not long after that, because Benedict has to stay until close, Ethan takes me home because I'm so drunk I can barely stand. It's not something that regularly happens, and while I don't tell them, it's because I'm trying to steel myself to read the letter from Nathan.

When we get back home, Ethan helps me get ready for bed, and once we're in my room I tell him I want to be alone. So he tells me goodnight and moments later, I'm sitting on the floor with Nathan's letter in my hands.

Shaky, unsteady hands open the seal and pull the letter out. And with what little strength and focus I have, I read it, holding my breath the whole time.

Caroline,

I want you to know, first off, how fucking sorry I am it came to this.

And second, I want you to know I intended to tell you everything when I came back from my trip. I was going to lay it all out and apologize for lying to you from the very beginning. I faced my past so I could make a better future, with you, but you see, long before we met...

I skip past where he tells me all about his wife and his life as Nicholas. I heard it all from the cops, I don't want to read it again, and look for where he starts talking about me and him again.

...I bought a ring and was going to propose, because I couldn't imagine the rest of my life without you.

Kind of like how I'm sure you're sitting here reading this, trying to comprehend how you're supposed to live the rest of your life without me.

Understand, please, that I'm leaving because I love you. Because I want to keep you and Rissa safe. And as long as I go back to who I was before, even if it's only in name and my own personal fucking hell, please know I would do anything to make sure my failures don't touch you or Rissa more than they have to.

I tried with her, I truly did. I went home to tell Roxanne I was finished, that I wanted a divorce, but she wasn't having it. God, after all this time, we were only married in name anyway. At least, I thought so, especially when I found out she'd moved on as well. But, when she revealed how much she knew, that's when I realized she would truly never let me go. To her, I was not and have never been more than a possession, and in her eyes, she owns me. It's one thing to suspect it, it's another to have it confirmed. I gave in because I felt like it was my only option, and she reminded me with a message saying she would kill me before she let me go right before I saw you tonight at the club.

So by the time you read this, I'll have left, and I know you'll be heartbroken. And while I'm sorry it ended this way, I'm not sorry we met, or that I love you. I wouldn't change a thing about any moment with you. I will never forget you. And I hope you know that.

One more thing.

There is no better moment than right now where I'm glad you met Benedict and fell in love with him. I know he won't fill the hole in your heart I'll be leaving behind, but please, don't push him away because of me and what I've done. I can tell he truly cares about you and in this fucked up world we live in, it's rare to find someone like that once, let alone twice. But you deserve it Caroline. If anyone deserves someone's love and devotion, it's you, even if you wonder sometimes why anyone loves you.

And I know you do. That's why I'm telling

you to embrace him, because he's everything you are, only in male form. And, if nothing else, I know you baby, and I don't want you to grieve long. I want your happiness more than anything else in the world.

Remember, every moment is precious. Don't waste a moment of it any longer. Figure out what you want and go for it. I'm sorry I will miss you getting everything you deserve out of life, baby.

And please, know in the end it wasn't any failing on your part here, but on mine. I will regret the fact it didn't end differently for the rest of my life.

I love you.

Always,
Nathan

I don't remember much after reading that.

I vaguely recall frantically searching through my things for something, anything of Nathan's to hold onto, which I will remember in the morning is something I don't have.

I barely remember curling up into a ball on my bedroom floor and howling with the overwhelming grief his letter brought back to the surface. Knowing he wrote that letter thinking he'd be alive — far away from me, and no longer in touch, but *alive*. And it just wasn't fucking right.

Everything I apparently tried to tell Ethan when he came into my room and held me; something else I don't remember.

But, in the morning, the remnants of my grief filled rage are gone from the room, the letter 'put in a safe place' according to Ethan, and my father is at the front door waiting for me to join him for brunch.

CHAPTER THIRTY-ONE

Brunch with my father is painful at first.

It's not that he doesn't care about me, or that I don't want to share, but the fact neither of us have really spoken about much of anything important in quite a long time. Yes, he's my father, but he's never really been my confidant, or even my friend. And as I poke at my food, he finally sets down his fork and sighs hard enough I tear my gaze from my plate to look at him.

Only to find him looking at me.

"I want to know how you're doing, Caroline."

Shrugging, my smile is self-deprecating as I lower my fork to my plate and let go of it. "I'm all right. Hungover, but that's about it."

"I won't tell you that you shouldn't drink like that, because I remember the days I did those sorts of things, but I hope you're not trying to drown your pain in a bottle. It's not a road that ever works out for anyone."

"No dad, I'm not. I rarely ever get drunk, which is something you would know about me if you—"

I catch my words because, after all, hadn't I recognized years ago that he loved me the best way he knew how? But he didn't miss the pain in my comment, or where I'm sure it's flashing in my eyes, and I don't miss his wince at the reminder about how much he failed as a parent in the love department. Even if he was better than my mother, who I'm glad isn't here today, as I'm sure I couldn't deal with her dramatics.

Yet, instead of getting tight-lipped and silent as he usually does, his hand reaches across the table for mine and covers it.

"Years before I met your mother, when I was a senior in high school actually, I fell in love with this amazing girl. She was a year younger than me, but we were very much in love, and had big plans. I graduated high school and went to college, she followed me a year later, and we became engaged. God, we adored each other, and I tried to convince her to run off and marry me without the huge wedding. She fought me for a bit, but after a while, seeing how everything cost so much and we made so little, we just decided to do it first and ask our parents for forgiveness later."

His story has my rapt attention, because he's never told me this, and a little dread sneaks in as I realize this story doesn't have a happy ending. "What happened?"

Following a squeeze of my hand, he sets it free and grimaces while leaning back in his chair. "We were only married two days when she passed away. She was only nineteen, but while we were out shopping, her eyes just rolled to the back of her head and she dropped to the ground. Her death was instant, and they told me later she died of an aneurysm."

My throat, clogged with emotion, reaches out for his hand and covers it. "I'm...I'm sorry."

"Thank you, but don't be. While it lasted, it was beautiful. And later, I found love again with your mother. It took me a while though, to open myself up to that sort of torture. Sweet as it is, when you lose it, however that takes place, it fucking hurts.

"But, love and grief don't have timetables, Caroline. The same for when you move on after you lose someone you love. And you knew Nathan almost four years. Just because he kept who he used to be a secret, doesn't mean you didn't legitimately love the man you knew him as. The few times we met, I could tell he truly loved you. You were a big part of his world and I'm more sad for you that he's gone than I'm mad at him for lying. Because while he was alive, you were so happy, and loved." He fidgets with something in his pocket, his eyes growing more sad by the second. "I wanted you to know that I've been there. I've hurt and I've recovered, and that's what I want for you. I want you to grieve, and then I want you to love again with your whole heart."

I want to say something, anything, but I can't. All I can do is feel how much he loves me, especially for him to tell me something that he obviously hasn't shared with many people in his life, and focus on how a little hole that's been hanging around in my heart starts to heal. I'm so overwhelmed I don't even notice the tears slipping down my cheeks until he reaches over and swipes one away with the pad of his thumb.

"You were such a lovely little girl, but as you got older, I knew less and less about how to connect with you. And I know your mother and you hardly ever saw eye-to-eye on anything. You pulled away and became this person I knew nothing about, and that's my fault, for not trying harder to get to know you, instead of trying to fulfill how inadequate I felt by buying you everything you wanted and more. But I want you to know I love you, no matter who you are, or who you love, or what you decide you want to do with your life. It's your life and all I want is for you to be happy."

"Daddy—"

"Wait. I want to give you something." He pulls his hand from his pocket and while keeping it closed, gives me an apologetic smile. "I lied to you, and at the time, I didn't know how important it was to you. You were so upset, when it broke I slipped it into my pocket, intending to get it fixed. I misplaced it and instead of admitting I lost it, I pretended I had no idea where it went. I'm sorry."

Opening his hand, there it is. The charm to my necklace, the one Benedict had given me, and the one I had cried so hard over. With a shaking hand, I lift it out of his palm, and into mine, closing my fingers around it as I hold it close to my chest with a soft cry of joy.

"There wasn't any way to repair the chain, but I knew that wasn't the important part, especially when I examined the charm."

Not having any idea what he means, I give him a confused look. "What do you mean?"

A genuine look of surprise flits across his face. "You've never looked on the bottom of the muffin? It's small, but there's a few words printed on it."

"No, I—I never knew." Wanting to know what it says, I lower my hand from my chest, roll the charm up into my fingers, and then instantly tear up as I see what Benedict had engraved on the bottom, reading aloud. "To hope. B."

"Who is B?"

I'm not sure how to answer him. I never told my mother and father about mine and Nathan's arrangement, thinking they wouldn't understand, and that it really wasn't something they needed to know. But seeing how he's trying right now to get to know me, to be closer to me, I have to hope I tell him and he understands.

"B stands for Benedict...and he's my boyfriend," I say while lifting my gaze to his once again. "He bought this for me for Christmas."

My father stares at me for a moment, his lips pursing a little in a way that tells me he's thinking before he speaks, and after a moment, he asks in a slightly amused tone, "So, you were what? In an open relationship?"

"Yes. We started dating about a month before Nathan died."

"I see."

"Do you?" Turning a little to get my purse, I open it and stick the charm inside one of the little pockets before turning back to my father with a raised brow. "You don't seem surprised at all."

"Actually, I always wondered. I saw you three once, walking down the street by that cafe I know you love as I drove by once, and you were talking on your phone. He held her hand and leaned over to kiss her on the lips."

I laugh at that, and damn, it feels good.

"I remember that day," I say to him with a smile. "It was about a month after Nathan and Rissa — that's her name — started dating. I had no idea you were nearby, let alone saw it. I never said anything because I didn't think—"

He holds up a hand to stop me. "It's all right. You didn't think I'd understand. I don't, really, but that doesn't mean anything. Were you happy? Because that's all that matters."

"Yeah, I was."

It's silent for a second, then he asks softly, "And now?"

"I think," I begin, going for complete honesty since he's asking. "I think I'm as happy as I can be given everything that's gone on. And it's getting better every day. Well, except last night. I finally read the note Nathan left me."

Tears surface even as I try to stay calm. He moves over a chair until he's sitting beside me, and knowing what I need before I even have to ask, envelops me in a tight hug. Leaning into him, I rest my head on his shoulder.

"I bet that was difficult," he murmurs near the top of my head, giving me a squeeze as I sniffle and nod. "I worried about you coming back here. Even though you acted normal, and although I haven't always been the most observant, I could tell you weren't really all right. You just got sick of me and your mother bugging you all the time."

An unexpected sputter of laughter bubbles out of me at his astute observation. "You guys were a little ridiculous."

"Not ridiculous." His voice is gruff, and I can tell he's getting a little emotional. "Just, trying to love you like you deserved, like we should've before this happened. I'm sorry, if you ever felt like we didn't because that's never been true. Not even for one damned second. You're the best part of our lives."

It's hard not to burst into tears at that, but I manage as I lift my head and say, "Thank you, dad. I...I love you."

"I love you too, sweetheart." He grins as I lean back into my own seat, crossing his arms over his chest as he asks, "So, this guy, is it serious?"

Returning his smile, I dab at my eyes with a clean napkin, and give a small nod. "Yes, we're pretty serious. It's been a little rough for us though."

He studies me, and his next question makes me wonder how he can read me so well. "What are you worried about?"

With a sigh, I explain to him about how

Benedict and I first met, what happened with Miranda and Len, and how I wasn't sure if I was going to be able to define my relationship with him. My father didn't say a word until I was done.

"Caroline, do you love him?"

"Yes."

"Does he love you?"

"Yes."

"Then what's the problem?"

I know this is a weird conversation for me to be having with my father, but I'm so glad he's listening to me I don't even really care. I decide to just lay it all out and see what he says.

"Miranda was the one who wanted to open the relationship. He did it for her and she betrayed him. I never planned to not have Nathan, you know? Now he's gone. I believe in open relationships, and I don't want to lose him because he doesn't want the same things as me. It's...it's so complicated."

"But it isn't." He laughs. "Have you even asked him what he wants?"

"No, because I'm afraid of the answer."

He lifts a hand, resting it on my shoulder after giving it a squeeze, and with a somber expression says, "You say you love him, prove it. Let him show you how much he loves you by trusting him enough to talk to him. And if there's anything I want you to take from this today, it's from my story. That plus Nathan's death just proves how you can lose someone in an instant, and because of that, you need to love as fiercely as you can. You'll never regret a moment of loving someone, Caroline; you'll only regret the moments you wasted on fears over something you have no control over. You got me?"

All I can do is nod as he pulls me into another hug, every single thing he said resonating with my heart, the one part in all of me that knows he's right and can admit it.

Now I just need to trust Benedict and our love for each other, and open my damn mouth.

It takes me a whole two weeks, but when we're finally able to spend a whole evening together, I work up the nerve to bring up the elephant in the room.

Where our relationship is at and where it's going.

I thought it would be easy, but as we sit in his living room after dinner, he's got a certain gleam in his eyes I've never seen before. When he starts to caress my bared skin on my shoulder, I realize it's a naughty glint, as if he has plans for tonight he can't wait to share.

"We need to talk," I begin, only for him to lean over and press a kiss against a sensitive part of my neck, causing me to gasp and stop talking.

He nips at my ear lobe with his teeth, then asks in a low voice, "Can we do it naked in bed?"

"Not sure you can be serious when we're undressed."

Drawing away, he makes sure we are looking at each other before he asks, "Serious? What's this about?"

"Us."

"Us?"

"Yes."

His lips quirk. "Okay, what about us exactly?"

Feeling the need to get up and move, I rise from my seat next to him and walk over to stand in front of the fireplace. I face it for a moment, then turn to find him staring at me with a neutral look on his face, and his arms crossed over his chest.

When I just stare at him, unsure how to begin, he asks, "Are we in jeopardy, Caroline?"

"Um." I pull my lip in between my teeth, biting down on it for a sec before letting go. "We might be."

His mouth flattens in a straight line, his body going rigid as he sits up straight, the desire in his eyes from our closeness moments before dying. "Why?"

"I'm not good at this," I admit, lifting my hands in the air as I shake them in a show of frustration, then drop them to my sides. "I'm afraid of saying the wrong thing and having you get mad at me for it even if it's not what I meant, and—"

"Whoa," he cuts in with a curt laugh. "Slow down. And give me some points for intelligence. Say what you need to say; I'm sure I'll get it just fine."

"Okay. Look. I—I never expected to not have him, okay?" I blow out a heavy breath and turn toward the fireplace again, figuring it will be easier to get the words out if I don't stare at Benedict as I talk, and raise my voice to compensate. "It was always going to be me and Nathan, as the core relationship, and then everybody else. And maybe that sounds terrible, but we were the center, y'know?"

"Yes, I know," he says in a softened voice as I pause. "You didn't plan for this."

"No, no I didn't. And so, I'm not sure what to do. And I... I read the letter he left me, two weeks ago, and saw my dad."

"You did?"

"Yes." I turn to face him with a sniffle. "I didn't tell you because I... the letter was hard to read, and my father... Well, he shocked me by showing up, wanting to take me out, but we talked. It was good."

He sits forward, clasping his hands together as he focuses on me. "I'm happy for you. I know how much you love your parents." He pats the seat beside him. "Come sit back down and tell me what's really going on."

"What's going on is I'm not sure we can stay together," I blurt out, and seeing him flinch at my abrupt statement almost makes me stop talking, but I figure I might as well just get it out. "I'm not like Miranda, okay? I would never do what she did to you, but I do believe in open relationships. And we both know you don't, not really. You're just not that type of person."

Benedict just stares at me, hands still clasped together, as he asks softly, "Why are you being such a coward?"

I can't believe he just called me that. "What?"

"You heard me." When I continue to stare at him with wide eyes, his voice is gruff as he asks, "I know the same things you do about him, Caroline. So, explain this to me. Why did Nathan break up with Rissa *before* his trip if he was planning to divorce his wife and live here permanently?"

"I don't know," I whisper, anxiety filling my chest as I take a step back when he stands up.

"Yes, you do." He advances on me, one slow step after another, but stops at least two feet away and asks again. "Why, Caroline?"

"I don't fucking know," I shout at him, my hands balling into fists at my sides.

"Yes," he returns with a rise of his own voice. "You fucking do. When did you figure it out? It had to've been the letter, because you didn't seem fazed by Rissa's statement at all. So, what was in the letter?"

"I don't know what you're talking about."

He growls, shoving a hand through his hair in clear frustration, and steps real close to me. Our faces are nearly touching as he says in his normal tone, "He might've loved Rissa, but he was in love with you. He was going to propose, Caroline. He believed in marriage and I'll bet you he believed in monogamy. But it's kind of hard to promise to be someone's one and only when you're already married, isn't it?"

"Shut up!"

I push at his chest, and his hands come up to hold onto my upper arms as he shakes his head, his eyes burning once more.

"No, because somebody needs to say it, so I will." He tightens his grip and makes sure his eyes are locked on mine before he puts into words everything I don't want him to. "He was going to tell you everything, he was going to propose, and then he was going to ask you to just be his. You know it, and I know it, and that simply fucking terrifies you, doesn't it? Because you don't want serious, Caroline. Even if he'd been straight up from the beginning, you were never going to meet his family, or make promises you didn't have to keep, or—"

"Fuck you," I shout at him, cutting him off, every inch of my body aching to give into the rage burning inside me. "You don't know anything! Let me go."

He does, stepping back with his hands lifted and palms out, lips flat in a grim disapproving line. "If I don't know anything, why are you so pissed off?" When I don't reply, he demands, "Look at me, Caroline. Look me in the face; tell me I'm wrong. Do that and I'll apologize."

I don't though, because I can't, and he knows it. We both do.

He's right and I can't deny it any longer, even to myself. One of the main appeals of being in a relationship with Nathan had been the fact he didn't want to be exclusive. Sure, we'd only been with each other the first few years, but it hadn't been on purpose; at least, I never thought it had. However, the more I thought about it after his letter these past two weeks, the more I realized he barely mentioned Rissa in the letter. Not that I doubt he did love her in his own way, but it certainly didn't meet the depth in which he loved me.

And it makes me sad because a part of me believes she deserved his devotion more than I did in some ways.

So we stand there, two people who love each other, but are stuck on opposite sides of the ocean-sized hole I placed between us months ago, and never really let go of. Never intended to, honestly, not deep down inside.

"You're not afraid of commitment, Caroline," Benedict says, his sudden statement loud in the near silent room as he slips his hands into his pockets, and I drop my eyes to stare at the floor. "Not as long as it's on terms you think you can live with, like being in an open relationship. But just you and him? If he proposed, what would you have said?"

I don't say anything, but that's okay, because he has lots to say.

"You would've said no, and we both know it. That's why you don't want to stay with me and only be with me. I don't give a fuck how our relationship began; it's turned into something else, and I'm not interested in sharing. And no matter how much you love me, how great things are between us, how amazing they could be if you would just give it a chance, you want to run away." He shrugs, his mouth turning down at the edges to make plain his disappointment along with his icy gaze, before he tears his gaze away and stares off to his side. "Well, go on then, leave. Run away."

"Benedict, I—"

"No," he cuts in with an angry swipe of his hand as he looks at me again. "You know, I realize you were genuinely upset Nathan died the way he did, and I know you truly grieve for him. However, you weren't all that upset at finding out about who he really was, and him having a wife, and now I know why. You were lying to him, and yourself, as much as he was lying to you. But you won't lie to me, Caroline. I won't allow it. And if you walk out that door, we're done. I won't chase after you."

The misery in his voice and in his eyes parallels the way I feel right now, as if my heart is being ripped in two. I want to tell him the truth, I want him to know he's right. I have all these things I want to say, but they won't come out like I need them to. Because when I met Nathan, I liked him enough to go along with what he suggested, especially because it's what I wanted. I can't know now why he suggested it then, but it must've been because he was married and in hiding, and unable to hope it would ever go anywhere.

I never meant for things to get so serious with him, but somewhere along the way it had, and I chose to willingly ignore it. It was silly and immature to assume we would skate along forever just living together and enjoying each other's company, with no expectations beyond that.

Expectations I know with everything inside me that Benedict has.

He wants marriage and a family. He thought he would have that with Miranda, but things changed.

He's ready for that. And me? I'm not sure I am.

I wish I did know. I wish I was ready. A part of me desires what Ethan and Destiny have, what my father talked about, and to let Benedict follow through on every single promise he's made to me every time he's looked into my eyes.

But in the end, a bigger part of me, the deep down fear of how inadequate I truly am is one I can't shake.

So, with a final whispered 'I'm sorry,' I gather my things and walk out the door, hating myself more and more with every step I take yet unable to stop.

CHAPTER THIRTY-THREE

Focusing on finishing the semester and graduating becomes my life.

Unwilling to examine my feelings or the choice I made, shoving everything deep down inside and locking it away is what I do, letting numbness take over and keep me going.

But it's not like I don't think about Benedict. It's kind of hard not to when I'm working in one of his clubs, even though I don't see him since I work with Felix and no one else. I avoid going to the club, or the cafe, or...okay, anywhere really. And I know it's dumb; hell I'm being dumb but I don't want to run into him. Or see him. Or talk to him. Not if I don't have to.

I can't stand when people are mad at me, or hurt by me, or disappointed in me. I don't want to see any of those things on his face, not after experiencing him looking at me as if I'm the only woman in the world. Mostly, I don't want to hurt him anymore, and staying away keeps us both safe from that happening. And he's kept his word; he hasn't chased after me. He hasn't called, he hasn't texted, and a tiny part of me fucking hates it even though it's exactly what I asked for by walking out.

I'm sure he had a small hope I'd change my mind by now.

I haven't even though I miss him so much it hurts, at least when I'm willing to acknowledge it, in the rare moments I let myself cry because I can't hold it in anymore.

So, it's been a long month so far, but I'm making it, day-by-day.

A hard tap on my shoulder makes me jump a little, bringing me back to reality as I sit in class, and I whip my head around to find a blond, shaggy-haired man with dark green eyes smirking at me.

"You all right?" He asks me this in a whisper, and when I nod my head while wondering why he cares, he continues with, "Just making sure. I tapped you like twice before you responded. Got a pencil I could borrow?"

"No, sorry."

"You sure?" He nods down at my backpack. "I saw you get yours out, you've got whole row of them. Please?"

"This is college, you should bring your own?"

Gosh, I'm being a bitch, but he doesn't seem to care.

"Is that a question?" Grinning, he holds out his hand. "Seriously, let me borrow a pencil. My sister is like, six, and she got into all my stuff and snapped them in half. I didn't notice till I was already here."

With a huff, because inside I kinda melt at him talking about his sister with such affection but don't want him to know that, I reach down and grab a pencil. Turning back to him, I hiss at him, "Don't stick it in your mouth or whatever people do. That's nasty and I don't want your mouth on my stuff."

"Don't touch anything to do with you, with my mouth. Got it."

"Are you hitting on me?"

He leans close, still whispering, and lifts a brow. "Do you want me to hit on you?"

"No."

"Then I'm not. Thanks for the pencil." He sits back and with a mischievous smirk, sticks the pencil in his mouth and bites down on it with his teeth. "Oops."

"Asshole," I mutter while turning back around to pay attention to what's left of the lecture, and he smartly doesn't say anything else.

But when class is over and I'm walking toward my car, he comes running up beside me and falls in step next to me without a word. I should probably be disturbed by this, but I simply ask him, "What are you doing?"

"You were nice enough to give me a pencil. I figure I should be nice and walk you to your car."

I refuse to look at him even though I can feel him every time he casts a glance at me. "I don't need you to come with me for that, but thanks. And you're welcome, even though I didn't give you the fucking pencil."

"Yeah you did. You handed it to me."

"You're annoying."

"Thanks. My sister tells me that all the time, and I almost forget every time that she's the six year old and I'm twenty-two."

I see my car in the not-so-far distance and reply to his friendliness with a little snark. "Well nice to meet you mister annoying, but I have to get going now."

"David," he says as he stops on the curb and gently grabs my arm to stop me from walking as well. "I'm David. And you're Caroline."

I jerk my arm from his, glaring. "I am? Thanks for telling me. I never would've known."

"Hey, I didn't piss in your cereal, I swear."

"Is there a reason you're bothering me, David? Did I look at you funny or something to make you think I wanted to chat or have a new friend?"

"No, but—" He sighs as I walk over to my car, unlock it, and open the door. "You're that girl, aren't you? The one whose boyfriend was murdered on New Years?"

Freezing, I snap, "What about it?"

I swear he's not fazed by my attitude at all, because he laughs at me, shrugging. "Nothing. You just seem really sad and I thought maybe you'd like to do something fun."

"Like a date?"

"Yes."

Wow, he must really be a glutton for punishment. My voice is incredulous as I ask, "Did you seriously wake up today and decide asking me out on a pity date was a good idea?"

"No." He drops his gaze from my face, to my blouse, down to my jean-clad legs, and then drags his eyes back up again with a grin. "No pity here. I think you're very attractive, actually. And I wanted to ask you out the first time I saw you but then I heard your name... and yah. I thought I should I wait a bit."

"So you placed an arbitrary time limit on how long you thought you should wait to ask me out because my boyfriend died and you wanted to make sure I got over my grief?"

I don't know why I'm continuing to stand here and banter with this guy, but then again, it's nice to feel amusement. Made even better by the fact he isn't bothered by my hostility, because he laughs again. And I hate to admit it, but I like his laugh and the fact he isn't put off a bit.

"You're a bit too serious," he says stepping closer until he's right by me again, the door of my car the only thing between us. "Therefore, you need to go out with me. We can get some food, go dancing? Something, anything, if it will make you smile because I can't decide if I like you completely until you smile."

I open my mouth to say no, but stop short when I wonder what the hell I'm doing. Isn't this exactly what I want? To date? To have fun? To not have people expect things out of me I feel incapable of dealing with?

"Okay, sure."

"But—" He blinks once, then again as he realizes I agreed instead of objecting, and says, "Awesome."

"You should meet me after work."

When he nods, I rattle off the address, and with his confusion clear asks, "Dancing it is, but why don't you work at the one close by?"

"It's for an internship so I go where I'm told and I'll already be there so." Okay so it's a half-truth but who cares. "Anyway, nine good?"

"Sure, I'll meet you there." He winks at me. "See you then."

He walks away and I get into my car, looking forward to doing something besides hanging out in my room this evening, and head home for a bit before work.

❧

ETHAN AND DESTINY get home about five, right as I finish making spaghetti for dinner, and we sit down to eat.

Living with them drives me insane, but since I want to leave this area when I'm finished with the semester, getting my own place would be a waste of time. And if my parents taught me anything, it's that you don't waste money just because you're annoyed.

It's not that I'm not happy they are happy; I guess you could say I'm jealous. It seems so easy for them, and it makes me question what's wrong with me, besides the obvious.

Destiny has less of an opinion of what happened with me and Benedict because we aren't really close, but not Ethan. I know he disapproves and thinks I'm making a huge mistake, even if he hasn't come right out and said it. I expect he will sooner rather than later. Like, right now when I tell him about how I'll be out late.

"So," I say after finishing my plate and standing up. "I'll be home late tonight. Just wanted to let you know so you don't worry."

"Doing extra work?"

"No. I have a date." I don't wait to see his reaction, turning on my heel and heading toward the kitchen. It's not even a few seconds before he arrives in the kitchen and stands with his arms crossed, blocking the door as I place my plate in the sink and face him. "What?"

"You know, I love you, but you're a fucking idiot."

I expected his irritation, so I'm able to keep my face neutral, but on the inside I flinch at his words. I don't want him to know how his opinion hurts my feelings, but I don't resist being a little bitchy in reply. "Shouldn't you be in the other room snuggling with Destiny? I didn't ask for your thoughts on my life or who I date."

"Seriously?" He steps closer, the scowl on his face deepening, and keeps coming until I'm backed against the sink. He's never done something like this to me, so I'm not afraid of him or anything, but the look of disgust on his face says it all even before his words do. "You're not the friend I know and have known my whole life. People's feelings aren't something you fuck with, Caro, and you need to knock it the hell off right now, before you push me and them all away for good."

"I'm not messing with anyone's feelings!" The words come out of me loud, practically a shout, and it's his turn to flinch as he takes a few steps back. But he doesn't get off that easy as I advance on him and stab him in the chest with one finger. "If I were messing with anyone's feeling, I would've stayed with him. I was being fucking honest by walking out on him!"

He goes the opposite way, snatching my hand in his, and giving it a squeeze as he whispers sadly, "You're not being honest though, Caro. You're afraid of how you feel and what it means for you two. You're running away."

Yanking my hand out of his, I step back and then around him, tossing him a glare over my shoulder. "Suddenly you're the expert on relationships? I'm so glad it worked out for you and Destiny like it has, but don't try and act like you have all the answers."

"There aren't any answers, Caro, because this isn't a fucking test or quiz. But if it were, you'd fail it. A big, fat, fucking F on emotional maturity, because if you were honest at all, you'd never have dated *either* of them in the first place."

I whirl on him with a growl of frustration, the

fight I didn't know I ached for landing right in my lap, and snap at him, "Oh, so now I'm supposed to have just fucking known Nathan's whole open relationship attitude was a cover? Fuck you."

"No!" He yells at me, throwing his hands up in the air, jerking them fast and hard in his annoyance, kinda like if he were holding onto my shoulders and shaking me. "If you don't know why anyone would date you, why anyone would love you, then don't fucking date them at all. If you can't love yourself, Caro, then nothing anyone ever does or no matter how much they love you, you'll never accept it. Even if you love them, if you can't receive as good as you give, then you need to quit before you keep making messes like this one."

I hate him in this moment for saying that, for baring how I feel to the conscious part of me, and as tears stream down my face and my hands clench at my side, I whisper, "Shut up. Just shut up."

"I can't," he replies in just as soft a voice, stepping close to me again, and sliding his arms around my shoulders. "Because I'm your friend and I care about you. I love you. And you have to love yourself, even when you don't want, or don't know how to do that." I let him bring me close to his body and hug me, even as my body stays rigid with all the emotions I can't manage to differentiate between, hands still in fists. "If you don't want Benedict because you truly don't want to stay with him, then fine, but otherwise, fight harder Caro. Nobody can do this for you."

"You read his letter, didn't you?"

It comes out as a question, but it's not.

"Yes," he says, sighing. "I know it was private, but I wanted to know what he said to upset you. And the thing is, I thought he was great for you before; now I'm sure he was even if you can't see it."

"Of course I see it." I lift my hands, pushing against his chest, and he releases me with another heavy exhale. "He was... perfect, even knowing all his secrets now. And even though I say I hate him for it, I don't." I swipe at my eyes to brush away the traitor tears and sniffle. "It killed me to read that and know if Nathan had lived, I might've broken his heart. Even if he thought I might turn him down, he didn't know for sure, but I do. And that makes me a terrible person."

"No, it doesn't." Ethan's face lights up in a ghost of a smile as he lifts his hand and strokes my cheek gently with the pad of his thumb. "And I think that you think you would've said no, but you truly loved him Caro. Remember what you said to me about a year after you started dating him?" When I shake my head, confused, he laughs. "You told me you'd never been so happy, that he fulfilled you in ways you didn't even know you needed. Doesn't sound like a person who would turn down a marriage proposal when it came down to it, does it? You were so tired though, I didn't even get to reply before you dozed off that night."

Suddenly, I remember telling him that, and in a daze, I find the closest chair and sit in it. I can't even say he's right because I don't know. Nathan never got to ask me to marry him, and now he never would. All I know is this argument has crashed through my numbness, bringing back all the pain I shoved deep down, and making me acknowledge how mine and Nathan's relationship changed every day from the start.

I might've been young, but he became everything to me. We got along so well, I can't remember a time we ever fought, and our lives just meshed. We fell naturally into our roles and I never questioned it; why would I? As long as I hadn't questioned it, my fears stayed hidden. I never had to admit to him how broken I felt on the inside, how unlovable I thought myself, but that letter proved he knew all along.

And I saw now how he tried to show me how much he loved me all the time, trying to reassure me without coming out and saying it.

I never felt for anyone like I did for him.

That is, until I met Benedict... a relationship I'm sure I've fucked up almost beyond repair.

What have I done?

Ethan watches me as I stand up, and as I turn to leave the room without saying anything else, he grabs my upper arm. I don't turn back to him though, even as he says, "I know you're gonna go out, and all I wanna say is, be safe Caro. And don't do anything you might regret later."

Instead, I nod as he releases me, and within a few minutes, I'm in my car heading to work as our conversation plays over and over in my head.

CHAPTER THIRTY-FOUR

The end of my work shift arrives, and with a half hour until David's arrival, I'm not sure what to do.

Should I stay, or should I go?

I haven't really decided what I'm going to do about Benedict. And me.

In all honesty, it really sucks that I haven't heard from him. Contradictory to how I should feel, I guess, because he's always been a man of his word. I asked for it. He told me the consequences if I walked, but I mean, how could he just let me go if he loves me so much? He waited for me eight months when I didn't speak a word to him, and I know it's different now than it was then, but he just let me walk out.

Yes, I know it doesn't mean he doesn't love me, or want to be with me. After all, I walked away, so that makes me just as bad. He wasn't unclear about his feelings after all. I'm the one who is so damned lost.

And here I've accepted a date, for what? Spite? To self-sabotage? Comparison?

I'm pissed at myself because I don't even know.

I liked David's tenacity though. He hadn't been put off by my attitude and I'm fairly sure he'd make a great friend if it comes to that. I need people who will put me in my place when I start acting like a raging bitch or have pity parties. Like Ethan, although he honestly held out longer than I thought he would.

In the end, I decide to be here when he arrives, because it's probably rude to just bail. Since I have to see him in class, for roughly another seven weeks, I'd rather not have things get awkward.

Heading to the restroom to freshen up, I exit again a few minutes later, and while walking back to the main dance area, I walk right into Felix because I wasn't watching where I'm going.

"Caroline," he says with surprise as I raise my gaze to his after he reaches out to steady me. "I thought you left."

"Not yet. I'm—" I lick my lips and glance around him real quick before returning my focus to him. "I'm meeting someone here tonight."

I can't be sure what emotion flashes over his

face, but it's gone quick as he asks, "Dancing with friends?"

"No. You're still holding me. You can let me go, you know."

"Sorry." He drops his hands like I'm burning his fingers and steps back after clearing his throat. "Well, I hope you enjoy your date."

Ah, I can practically hear the disapproval in his tone now. "Thanks, I will. Immensely."

"I was married once," he says in a low voice as I walk around and past him, stopping me in my tracks. "We met when we were both eighteen, married right out of college, we were crazy about each other from the day we met." He pauses, but I don't have to ask what happened, because he offers it right up, his statement full of a sorrow he hides so well. "Then, a year and a half ago, after six years together, she died."

"I'm sorry." And I am. I know how bad it hurts.

"So am I. And I know we're not friends which means I'm supposed to mind my own business when it comes to your personal life, but I can't. When my wife died, I thought I would never recover. Some days I still wake up having dreamt of her, rolling over to hold her close, only to discover she isn't there. I do nothing but work, hoping it will get me through one more day. I can't talk to a new woman in more than a platonic way, or go on dates, and other than my therapist, I've never admitted this out loud. But I'm afraid to move on because with all it entails, my biggest fear isn't loving someone else, because she would want that for me; she would want me happy."

He stops with a sigh, and then speaks again, the humor in his voice tinged with sadness. "No, my fear is that kissing another woman will make it so I won't be able to remember what the last kiss my wife ever gave me felt like anymore."

Turning around slowly, I lift my arms and cross them over my chest, frowning at him as I quickly do the math. "How old are you? Thirty?" When he nods, I say without thinking, "You're too young to spend the rest of your life alone."

His smile turns into an amused, and knowing, one as he slides his hands into his pockets. "Takes one to know one?"

"Not really. Doesn't seem like you struggle to love yourself."

"Ah, is that what you think?" He shrugs, glancing away for a moment before looking back at me, and smirks. "I got lucky. My wife loved me even when I didn't love myself, and I appreciated her every day for it. Her and her stiff upper lip got us both through a lot of moments of crisis in our lives."

Our first conversation makes sense now. "That's why you would go to England."

"Yes, but only because that's where we first met. Our lives, our memories, they are all here in the house we lived in together. Some days I wonder if it would be better if I didn't live there anymore; if I didn't hear her laughter in every room, every time I enter them. Doesn't matter though. I'm unwilling to give up that piece of her."

My eyes tear up and I look down, asking, "Why are you telling me this?"

"Because." I feel him step closer until we're nearly touching, and then his hand is under my chin, gently tilting my face up until he's staring into my eyes with his own pain filled ones. "My wife, in one of my moments where I questioned why I was even breathing, once told me something I'm going to tell you right now. And that is... you are enough. You are worth every breath you take, and every person you love, and every person who loves you, and every single hand that holds yours. You deserve every moment of happiness you get, and you also deserve for someone to hold you when you are down, and let them love you through the pain."

My breath hitches as he brushes the pad of his thumb across my cheek. "And as to what I would add to that? What you do, who you love, how quickly you love them? That's nobody's business but yours. And even if you don't love yourself, even if you've never loved yourself, you should let others love you, and appreciate every second of it. You have an advantage, Caroline. There's a man, one of my longest standing friends, who fucking adores you like I adored my wife, and all he's waiting for is you to knock on his door."

"You don't know that," I whisper, my lips trembling with my barely suppressed emotions at how his words resonated through every inch of me and my fragile heart. "I don't deserve to knock on his door. I walked away even though I knew it was wrong the whole way."

"Trust me, he already knows your fear overrode every other part of you. So do us all a favor, and go put the man — and yourself — out of misery, for all our sakes. Stop wasting the one thing none of us ever get back, no matter how hard we wish we could. Time."

I hear him, just like I heard Ethan earlier, and even though it won't get rid of a lifelong lack of self-love, I give in to what I want. To what I desire. To what I need.

And what I need in my life is Benedict, for however long it lasts. However long we have.

Hopefully, with enough love surrounding me, I can manage to do the one thing I should've been doing all along: loving myself.

Whatever Felix sees in my eyes makes him grin, and before I can say anything, he leans down and presses a short, firm kiss to the corner of my mouth. I don't know why he did it, but I don't ask. I tell myself it's because we can connect over something not many people can, and he's trying to comfort me; give me an extra touch of strength to go do what I need to do. He pulls back as I sigh with and says with a chuckle, "Don't tell him I did that."

"I won't," I say as he lets me go, but then grab his arm as he goes to turn away to say one last thing. "Thank you, Felix. And just so you know, I don't think you'll ever forget her, or her laugh, or her kiss, because it's clear those are etched in your heart and your memories. I'll... I'll see you next week."

I don't wait for a response. I turn and take off at a run toward the entryway to the club, only to stop when I get near the entrance because David is standing there against a wall. His eyes search the room, surely looking for me, so I step into his line of vision, and his face lights up when he catches sight of me. Walking toward him, I stop a bit in front of him, and try not to look down at my feet nervously.

His first comment is rather astute considering we don't know each other that well. "Something tells me you're about to leave when I've just gotten here."

"Yeah, I am—"

"I'm sorry," he cuts in with a frown. "I shouldn't have acted like that earlier."

"Nah." I shake my head, smiling at him with genuine friendliness, which makes his eyes go wide. "You didn't do anything wrong. I'm just... in love with someone I really need to go apologize to."

"Figures." He pouts, lip sticking out along with his puppy dog eyes, before he shrugs as if it doesn't matter and laughs, his gorgeous green eyes practically dancing with humor. "Woman as beautiful as you actually being single? I expected you to turn me down flat out."

"Well, can't be mad at a guy for having the guts to ask in the face of rejection." I smile at him again and say, "I'll see you in class tomorrow, right?"

"Yep. See you then." After I walk around him and am about to exit, he calls out to me. "Hey. Hope everything goes well."

"Thanks," I say with a glance over my shoulder at him before turning back around and taking off at a run to my car.

I don't know if he's at work or home, but I figure work is the place to start, and with a quick text to Ethan that I 'changed my mind' about the date and nothing more, I head to the other club.

CHAPTER THIRTY-FIVE

Benedict wasn't at the club, something Frank instantly informed me the moment he saw me, and told me he took the night off. He offered to send him a message, but I said no, and he seemed to understand I wanted to surprise him. I probably should've had Frank ask where he was and what he was up to in a casual manner, but instead I just took off and headed to his house.

So, here I am pulling into his driveway, sighing with relief at seeing his car in the driveway and knowing he's inside. Shutting off my car, I take a few deep breaths, then get out of the car and head toward the door. The motion sensor porch light comes on as I climb the steps, and after another slow intake of air in and out, I press the doorbell.

I'm almost about to press it again after waiting

for what is probably no longer than thirty-seconds, but feels like forever, when he opens the door.

The moment his eyes land on my face, he keeps one hand on the door, and the other drops to his side as he simply says, "Oh, it's you." His face gives nothing away; it's the neutral Benedict, the one I rarely had focused on me. And at first, I can't say anything, I'm just so happy to see him, my eyes slowly taking him in from head to toe. And he looks good enough to eat in a white button down with the top two unfastened to give a glimpse of the golden skin underneath, tucked into his black suit pants, and his sock covered feet. I lift my gaze back to his face, where his face hasn't changed from its curious but detached countenance.

He might be hiding his feelings, but I know mine are plain to see. I feel every single one humming through me as my stomach clenches with anxiety, and my heart squeezes, trying to prepare for the rejection I know could possibly happen. I'm not counting anything out since I know I probably deserve to be turned down after the way I just walked out.

Bad with words, not wanting to mess up, or screw up what I came to say, I keep my eyes locked square on his and announce, "I'm here to grovel."

His eyebrows shoot up as he clears his throat and then frowns. "Caroline—"

"Please," I practically beg, stepping into the frame of the door. "Let me say what I came to say."

Not replying, he merely steps back with a nod, and once I'm inside, he shuts the door. Crossing his arms over his chest, he quirks one brow and looks at me expectantly.

I rush to speak, letting the words tumble out of me as if I am about to run out of breath for good, shoving my fear away for what I hope is the final time.

"I fucked up," I begin, clasping my hands in front of me with what I hope is a contrite look on my face, my eyes carefully watching for the moment I hope he thaws and smiles at me like I want. "Before you, all I knew was Nathan. From the start, I thought he and I wanted the same things. I can't change that. I know I had nothing to do with what he truly had going on, and I only knew what he showed me, but he never made me compromise. We just were who we were, from the very beginning, and when I met you, it was on my terms really. Nothing was supposed to end up like this, but it has, and for someone who never had to compromise, it was like being slapped in the face."

I pause for second, and when he just keeps waiting with his stony face, I press on with what now feels like a confession. I guess in a way it is. "I went along with him no matter what he wanted, and then he met Rissa, and then...then I met you. And I've never felt so strongly for anyone in my life, other than him. It was weird, but you just...you reached a part of me he hadn't. You expected nothing of me, you eased one of my fears — about gifts — without me even telling you about it first. I never meant to hurt you. You know, I never hurt Nathan," I admit with a wobbly smile. "I'm not sure I could've hurt him with anything I did, ever. He knew I'd never leave him and I know if he had truly been who he presented himself as, he never would've left me. We were as solid the day he died as I told myself we were the day I met you, and his death forced me to let him go in a way his simply leaving wouldn't have allowed me to do."

A tear trickles down my cheek and I swipe it away before continuing. "I can't change the way I feel about myself overnight. But you? I love you, and if you think I'm worth your love and devotion, I'll work every day to believe it myself. Even if you make me feel vulnerable, even if knowing that letting you all the way in will cause so much hurt if it doesn't work out, I have to. I want to receive love as well as I know how to give it, and I want it to be with you. Because the idea of not having you in my life at all sucks worse." I reach for the chain on my neck, the one I bought and put the muffin charm on, and lift it so he can see. "My father had the charm, he gave it to me months ago, when I saw him. I've had it ever since, but I couldn't put it on my neck 'til now. Until I deserved it."

The softening of his face has me taking a step forward, but he lifts a hand to halt me, and shakes his head. "I can't—"

Unable, and unwilling really, to hear him turn me down, I launch myself at him with a sob. He catches me and wraps me in his arms, even though his footing stutters for a second before he's standing firm again, and I wrap my arms around his neck as I pretty much babble, begging and pleading with him. "God, please, don't send me away. I'll get whatever help you think I need, and when I want to run away, I want you to make me stay because sometimes I might not be strong enough. But I don't want to leave you, and I think sometimes I just need you to remind me you won't let me go, no matter how badly I fuck up. And god, I miss you, I miss couches, I miss you fu—"

"Shut up." His lips on my mine cut off my words, swallowing my small mix between a laugh and sob at his words into his mouth, and I open to let his searching tongue in. A groan of pleasure from each of us, the tightening of our arms around one another, and without warning he backs me into the door.

A gasp rips through me at the force of it, but an

even bigger one escapes when someone — someone fucking *female* — lets out a soft laugh, and I rip my mouth from his as he groans as if he's been caught with his hand in the damned cookie jar and growls out, "Fuck."

"So sorry, Ben." She laughs again. "Wondered where you went; now I know."

"What—?" I can't see anyone over his shoulder and I push at them with both my hands. "Put me down!"

"I tried to warn you," he mutters, letting me go so my feet meet the floor gently and then turning so I can see who walked in, but he instantly introduces us. "Caroline, meet my mother. Mom, Caroline."

Oh, hell. I feel myself blanch even as my cheeks flush, forcing some attempted polite words past my lips even though I want to go hide in embarrassment and anxiety. "Oh, hi. I...uh...we..."

"Dear lord son, hold onto the girl before she passes out and hits the floor." His mother gives me a sympathetic smile as Benedict wraps his arm around my waist and pulls me close to his side, and then it turns into a pure smile of joy as a man enters the hallway and she says, "Honey, you know that woman Benedict keeps rattling on about? She's here!"

When he steps up to her side and looks our

way, it's clear these are Benedict's parents. Not only because she called him 'son,' but just by looking at them, I see his face in both of theirs. And even though I'm nervous, I give them a tremulous smile while trying to calm my nerves.

"Nice to meet you," I manage to say, not imagining the heavy sigh of relief Benedict takes beside me. Did he think I would be rude? Not a chance, not after he just had his tongue in my mouth. "I'm sorry to just show up—"

"No need to worry about it, sweetie." She waves a hand in the air and laughs again, with a lyrical quality I enjoy. "It's about time for us to go anyway. Darling, did you call the cab?"

"I was just about to call," his father says, all eyes on his wife, before he turns them on his son. "I know you were going to take us to the airport, but looks like you've got company now." Then, his gaze travels to my face, and his smile is as beautiful as his sons. "Nice to meet you, too, Caroline. We look forward to getting to know you, but that time is not right now. We're about to go on our anniversary trip."

Clearing my throat, I find my voice and say, "Oh, wow, congratulations. I hope you have fun."

"Oh, we will." His mom says that as his father walks off while dialing the phone after nodding at the both of us. "I should go get my things." She steps closer and closer until she's standing right in front of us, leaning in to hug Benedict and kiss him on the cheek, then pulls back and turns to me. "I assume we'll be seeing lots of you in the future now?"

"Mom." Benedict's voice is filled with warning and not-so-hidden amusement. "Please."

"Okay, okay," she says with another cheerful smile as she steps back. "I'll let you know we get there safely, because you know your father will forget. Don't want you worrying about us."

"All right." He calls out, "Have fun, Dad."

When he doesn't respond, his mom gives a waggle of her fingers in farewell and spins on her heels, heading toward wherever her husband went. After a glance down at me, Benedict grasps my hand in his and practically drags me up the steps and into his bedroom, shutting the door behind us.

"Get naked," he commands, making the door click as he presses the lock, and then starts unbuttoning his shirt as I stare at him silently. "Right now."

"Aren't we going to talk?"

He shoves the shirt down and off, then unfastens his pants with a flick of his fingers, staring at me the whole time. "Do you have anything else you needed to say?"

"Uhm, no, I guess not."

"Then take off your fucking clothes, Caroline."

I would say I can't believe he doesn't need any more words between us after what I've done, but I absolutely do. Yet, I stand here frozen as he strips down until the only thing between his bare skin and mine is the space between us, and the clothing I still haven't removed. So, he stalks toward me, grabs me around the waist and lifts me off the ground, then carries me to the bed and lies me upon on it. I unfreeze as he pulls my skirt and panties down my legs, managing to get my shirt up and over my head to toss it aside moments before he spreads my legs and climbs up on the bed between them.

He aligns our bodies so he's completely covering me, lowers his mouth to my jaw, and begins showering me with soft, wet kisses; back toward my ear, up to nip at my earlobe with his teeth, and then down along my neck to my shoulder.

"I feel weird," I whisper as he starts to kiss down onto my chest, both his hands cupping a breast in each hand, and giving them a squeeze before closing his mouth around one nipple which begged for his attention. "Your parents are still here."

"Well," he says around my nipple, his breath

causing it to tighten more, "guess you better be real fucking quiet then, huh? I like that idea."

"Can't we wait till they leave?"

He shakes his head, not replying as he sucks harder on the one nipple while pinching the other between his fingers, fingers rubbing as if he's tried to roll it, and I whimper. I'm not sure how long he stays like that, simply worshipping my breasts, going back and forth between them, but it feels like forever.

Long enough I find myself joking as I prop myself up on my elbows to look down at him, "I think this is longest we've ever spent on foreplay."

Releasing the suction on one nipple with a pop, he lifts his gaze to mine as one hand begins traveling between our bodies, skimming along my stomach until he slides it between my thighs. Slipping his hand down, his fingers find me, wet and waiting for him to give me what we both want, what we both need.

"You deserve to be tortured a little, Caroline," he says while inserting one finger into me, making me gasp and drop back down to the bed as my eyes slam shut at the exquisite feeling. "I'm going to stay just like this, teasing your nipples with my mouth while fucking you with one finger only, getting you close only to deny you, until you can't be quiet any longer. How long can you hold out, sweetheart?"

"Not long." The words are weak, his simple touches as he does what he just said turning me on to the point of pain, and I wiggle my lower body to beg for him to give me what I want. "Simply being in the same room as you puts me on the edge of coming. Please, please..."

"You wanna grovel, Caroline? Beg me harder. Fucking beg me to give you what you want," he orders with a quick flick of his thumb over my clit and a curl of his finger inside me, only to stop completely a second later. "Now, or I'll leave you here aching for me, and go take a cold shower."

"Okay." It comes out as a wail as he sucks my stiff nipple with his mouth, flicking his tongue back and forth over it while his fingers stroke the sweet spot inside of me in a slow enough way my body can only hover on the cliff and not tip over. Lifting my hands, I slip my fingers into his hair and grip it best I can while lifting my lower body into his touch. "I'm sorry, so fucking sorry. I'll do whatever you want, just fuck me dammit."

"That's not begging, that's demanding." His words don't match the movement of his fingers as he slips a second finger inside and speeds up his stroking, his tone softening. "And I forgive you, Caroline, of course I do. I love you. I know you. And I knew you would be back. Now, tell me how much you want me inside you, love."

My chest feels like it's going to burst with all the emotions, enough so tears trickle down my cheeks unchecked, and it's all I can do to plead softly, baring myself heart and soul. "Please, you're what I want. I need you deep inside me, fucking me so hard and fast I can't breathe, and so slow and sensual I can feel every second how much you love me, and if you don't fuck me right now, I'm never gonna be the same—"

His touch leaves me, but not for long as he moves back on top, covering my body as his mouth captures mine. Wrapping my legs around him, he uses one hand to guide himself to me as the other entangles itself in my hair, his tongue tangling with mine at the same time he enters me with a hard thrust. It's all I need, and he captures my scream in his mouth as I come around his cock, my pussy clenching him deep inside me as my legs tighten around him, keeping him as close as I can.

Slowly moving as my body goes limp, he keeps my mouth trapped underneath his while making love to me, quiet as he can manage. But when we hear the door close downstairs, he rips his lips away, straightens so he's on his knees while still inside me, and lifts my legs straight up until they are over his shoulders.

No words are spoken, just pants, and moans,

and gasps from both of us as he grips my hips and fucks me hard and fast until we both can't breathe.

Until another orgasm even stronger than the last one makes me sob with joy, and he comes with a final slam of his cock, our bodies as close as two people could be.

And as our bodies cool and our heartbeats slow, he takes me into his arms so I'm lying on top of him, tucks my head under his chin, and murmurs, "I missed you, too."

"Really?" Sleepy, muttered sarcasm, but with no bite. I just want to bask in his warmth, in his gentle hold on me, but I'm unable to resist the urge to tease him. "I couldn't tell."

"Mmm, you should shut up before I put something in your mouth to make you."

"Already? Give me five minutes."

"We've got our whole lives," he says.

Or so I think he did.

I can't be sure, because I fell asleep, secure in the knowledge that while everything might not be perfect, it was exactly what I needed it to be.

"Where are you taking me?"

I ask Benedict this question as we walk through the mall on Christmas Eve and he just looks down at me with a mischievous smile. I don't know where we're going, but I know I can trust him.

It's been a little over two years since I showed up at his house and we've been taking it day-by-day, while still slowly building our future together. I went into counseling almost instantly after that to deal with things I should've dealt with a while ago, and we also went into couple's counseling; not because we were falling apart, but because we wanted to grow together and communicate in the best way we could, for us.

I graduated college at the top of my class, and

obviously, I didn't leave town. I really hadn't ever wanted to, but my reaction to pain was something I learned to control, so it wouldn't take over my life. My reactions weren't rational, and now when I get upset or hurt I instantly talk about it with whoever is hurting me, even though it takes courage every time.

Instead, Benedict launched another club — well, we did, since we both own it — and I took the job as manager since its grand opening a year ago. I love it, and of course the first thing we did in my office before opening was christen the couch, and my desk, and the floor. As for moving in together, that happened only six months ago; up until that point, I had continued living with Ethan and Destiny, who were more than happy to have me for as long as I wanted to stay. And honestly, it was nice to live around people I could have fun with; I think living on my own would've made me unhappy, so I didn't even bother.

They'd be lying if they said they weren't happy I finally left though. They were ready to get married and start a family since Ethan got a great job real close to where they lived in the city while Destiny worked from home. In fact, they were getting married tomorrow, just a little over three years after they met, and I still had to get a dress which is why we'd come to the mall tonight.

When Benedict comes to a stop, it jars me out of my thoughts as I pause beside him, and then look up at the store sign. We're standing in front of my favorite store, Charlotte Russe.

"Come on," he says while tugging on my hand. "Let's get you a new dress for tomorrow, and then we've got one more place to go."

"Okay!"

I follow him with a squeal of delight, and of happiness really, because I've been talking about a dress I've wanted for weeks now. And he just proves how amazing he is when he talks to the sales lady, she leads us to a dressing room, and inside is the dress in my size, along with matching shoes, making it clear he called ahead.

He leans against the mirror after we shut the door, arms crossed over his chest, and gives me one simple command while his eyes fill with a fiery desire that's all for me. "Strip."

I do, not that it's hard, considering I'm wearing my normal ensemble of a blouse, a skirt, and heels. I don't even bother with pantyhose, and haven't in a long while, since Benedict made it clear he wants to take me anywhere he can. And he has, many times; it has basically become a regular game between us. High risk places like dressing rooms, where we play his game: he fucks me hard and fast, and I'm not allowed to make a sound.

Let's just say, even though I'm pretty good at it, there's a couple times where my whimpers and moans have almost gotten us busted.

Once I'm standing in just my underwear, he helps me into the dress, which I have to put on over my head, and I stand in front of the mirror with him behind me after he zips it up.

"Beautiful," he murmurs into my ear, kissing my neck while keeping our gazes locked in the mirror, and I have to agree with him.

My hair goes well with the muted, yet luscious soft yellow of the dress. It's a strapless dress, with a v-cut in the bosom of it, the top smooth and silky. Around the waist is a sash in a slightly darker, yet just as gorgeous color, and then the dress puffs out almost like a ballgown but not as big. The tiny layer of ankle-length petticoats underneath are soft, and will most likely make a soft swish sound when I walk, while having the added effect of making me feel incredibly sexy.

He gathers the skirt at the edges while I watch, slipping his hands underneath once it's high enough, and shimmies my panties down my legs.

"What the hell," I hiss, stepping out of them all the same as he kneels at my feet. "I need those."

"Nah." He slips them into his pocket as he stands back up and grins at me in the mirror as he says, "Shoes."

Sighing at his antics, I slip into the heels that match the sash, and once that's accomplished, he growls while procuring a store bag out of what seems like thin air. "Put your clothes in this and let's go."

"I can't just walk out of here wearing this!"

"Yes you can. I paid for it earlier." He chuckles as my mouth drops open and walks over to the bench, picking up my clothes and shoving them into the bag, then opens the door. "Much as I'd love to fuck you right here while you're in that, we gotta get going. So come on."

I blush as the associate, who had been walking by at the same time, busts out into laughter, and exit the store moments later to her cheerful farewell, "Have a nice evening and a Merry Christmas!"

Not even a minute later we're entering a store I've never heard of, and we're in another dressing room before I can even gather what the hell we're doing here. But I certainly won't complain since he's stripping down right in front of me, and then, a knock at the door before a few items of clothing are hung over the top.

"Thank you," Benedict calls out before grabbing a pair of jeans and putting them on, turning around so I can see him buttoning them in the mirror, and of course my focus goes to his ass.

He smiles knowingly as I step up behind him and cup one side in each hand, giving the cheeks a squeeze, and then slide my hands around to rest on his bare stomach. It's not the first time I've seen him in jeans, but he's been saying he needs some new pairs since he began wearing the ones he had more often at my request, we might've ripped a couple in our constant haste to take them off. And god, does he look even more tasty in jeans, so much I want him to fuck me right here.

"Stop looking at me like that, or I'm going to lift your skirt and—" A kiss on his shoulder blade makes him cut off with a hiss, one that extends when I nip at his skin with my teeth, and he fists his hands at his side while saying through clenched teeth, "We can't have sex right now. We need to get somewhere important."

"It's been a while since we did it in a dressing room, are you sure?" I back away from him and he watches me in the mirror. I drop my hands to my own sides, lifting up my skirt in a slow tease while continuing to back up until my back is against the opposite wall, and spread my legs slightly. "You know you want to touch me."

"Caroline, put your skirt down." His words say one thing, his eyes say another, as does the arousal straining against the jeans to be set free.

"Why the hurry?" Careful to bunch the skirt in one hand but not crunch it, I bare my pussy to his eyes in this tiny little room, and glide my own hand between my legs. I close my eyes since I know he won't take his eyes off me, and focus on enjoying all the sensations these little escapades always give me, whimpering with excitement as I slip a finger inside myself. "Mmm. This should be your hand."

My breath hitches as I add another finger and curl to stroke my g-spot, running my thumb over my clit to send licks of pleasure humming through my body, and I bite my lower lip to keep myself from making any noise at all.

It's faint, but I hear him pop the button on his jeans, which makes me release my lip from the grip of my teeth to grin in triumph. I don't open my eyes though. Soon he has a hand on the outside of each of my thighs, and he places a kiss on the back of my hand, the one I'm using to pleasure myself.

His breath is hot as he declares, "My turn. Get your fucking hand out of the way of my mouth."

"Go ahead," I say breathlessly, removing my fingers with a soft laugh. "And please, tell me what victory tastes like while you're at it."

His chuckle vibrates against me as he dives in after cupping my ass with both hands and lifting me for better access. My hands grip his hair while I enjoy every lick of his tongue, every small graze of his teeth against my clit, and his ever tightening grasp on my ass as he pleasures me.

My whole body goes taut in preparation for my impending orgasm, but when an 'oh god' slips out of my mouth and into the air around us, he pulls away, leaving me hanging. He doesn't make me suffer though; oh no, he wouldn't dare, not with the way I'm gripping his hair like I'll die if I let go.

He stands up until he's trapped me against the wall, angles my hips, and says, "This is what victory tastes like."

I taste myself as his mouth captures and invades mine, his cock thrusting into me so hard the whole store would've heard me scream without his first action, and I'm grateful for it. I would hate for this to be interrupted. We stay like that, our tongues tangling, him thrusting as hard as he possibly can while not making the wall of the changing room so much as quiver, until I'm hovering on the edge of my orgasm again...and he fucking stops.

"Fuck," I hiss while still trying to keep my voice down, bucking my hips as he smirks at me. "What the hell is wrong with you? If you're in such a hurry, you should've gotten me off by now."

"I'm not in a hurry. I just had plans for us this evening, and now you've derailed them."

My hands slip from his hair to his shoulders, resting there as he pulls out to the tip, and then digging in when he shoves himself all the way in again, and buries his face in the crook of my neck. Biting down on my lip barely keeps the moan inside me, and all I can think about is how much I love this man.

And how I wish he would take the next step, the one I'm finally ready for.

But, after he joked with our counselor a year ago that he was 'waiting for me to propose' when she asked if and when we had any plans to marry, I seriously have wondered ever since if he'd actually been serious. We did lots of things on my timeline because of my issues, but I have to admit I want him to get down on one knee and ask me, surprise me. However I don't want to wait any longer, and even if he thinks I'm joking, I want to say it. Let him know it's okay.

"Hey, Benedict?"

Out to the edge, and a thrust. A gasp from me; a moan from him, followed by him going, "Hmm?"

"Um, I'm just wondering…I think since I keep putting us in compromising positions, I should probably make an honest man out of you. Don't you think?"

His head shoots up and rears back, his hands gripping my ass so hard I'm sure it's gonna bruise, and his eyes go wide as he stares at me, his next words incredulous. "What the hell did you just say?"

Now unsure, I give him an innocent look. "What do you think I said?"

"Wow." He shakes his head like he can't believe it, then laughs, his whole body radiating his happiness as he wraps his arms around me and hugs me close. "Trust you to ruin my plans by beating me to it!"

Aw, shit. "We can pretend I didn't say it," I whisper as he pulls back to gaze down at me. "I thought you were waiting on me to say something—"

"Sweetheart, you're absolutely fucking amazing, so no, we can't pretend you didn't say it." Lowering his face close to mine, he presses one, then two soft kisses on my lips and smiles against my mouth. "My answer is yes. Fuck yes." He thrusts his hips, flexing his cock so I feel him inside me, and chuckles as my oversensitive nerves make me gasp because I'm so near to coming. "And my dick approves."

I can't help it; tears trickle down my cheeks at realizing we're engaged, and I don't want to run away from it. Or him. Ever.

And it's such a joy, to have come so far, that I

cup his face in my hands and say, "I love you," over and over as I shower kisses on his face.

"I love you too," he manages to reply once as I feel him lower us to the floor. "And what do you say we finish this real quick so I can take you home, fuck you again in our bed, and give you the ring I bought, hm?"

"Mm. It's not a muffin ring is it?"

He laughs. "No. But I might've inscribed 'I wanna eat your muffin forever' on the inside of it." He says this as he pulls again to the edge, and when I lift my head off the floor a little to stare at him with a mix of horror and amusement, he gives me a 'gotcha' look, and plunges right back in.

Fast and hard, I keep my legs locked tight around him, and as my orgasm takes over, our lips meld and mesh and make love to each other to the last second when he stiffens, his body coming softly down to cover mine while we try and catch our breath.

A gentle knock on the door makes us both jump up before we're ready as the sale associate asks, "Do you need any assistance?"

"God no," Benedict manages to say. "I just thought the pants were too big for a second, but I'm all right."

I cover my mouth with both hands to smother the peals of laughter just begging to get out, and he quickly changes back into his original clothing. Then, grabbing one of my hands as the associate says, 'okay' and walks away, he lifts it to his mouth and kisses the back of it.

"Ready?"

The question he asks is so simple, and yet, quite loaded.

He might be asking if I'm ready to go home, but in my heart, I'm answering it in more ways than one.

Ready to go home, yes.

Ready to finish healing, yes.

Ready to take the next step, yes.

Ready to pledge my life and my heart to him and become his wife before long?

"Yes." I squeeze his hand with mine, the word filled with so many promises we are both aware of, and step up on tip toe to brush his lips with mine. "Let's go home."

And we do, discussing our forever the whole way, however long that may be.

All I know is, I won't take a moment of it for granted ever again.

<u>THE END!</u>

**Thanks so much for reading! I hope you enjoyed Caroline and Benedict's love story! If so, please